A TIME TO WED

ELLIE ST. CLAIR

CONTENTS

Prologue	1
Chapter 1	7
Chapter 2	15
Chapter 3	22
Chapter 4	31
Chapter 5	43
Chapter 6	50
Chapter 7	61
Chapter 8	71
Chapter 9	76
Chapter 10	83
Chapter 11	91
Chapter 12	100
Chapter 13	103
Epilogue	111
An excerpt from A Time to Love	117
Also by Ellie St. Clair	123
About the Author	127

♥ **Copyright 2022 Ellie St Clair**

All rights reserved.

This book or parts thereof may not be reproduced in any form, stored in any retrieval system, or transmitted in any form by any means—electronic, mechanical, photocopy, recording, or otherwise—without prior written permission of the publisher.

Facebook: Ellie St. Clair

Cover by AJF Designs

Do you love historical romance? Receive access to a free ebook, as well as exclusive content such as giveaways, contests, freebies and advance notice of pre-orders through my mailing list!

Sign up here!

Also By Ellie St. Clair

To the Time of the Highlanders
A Time to Wed
A Time to Love
A Time to Dream

For a full list of all of Ellie's books, please see
www.elliestclair.com/books.

PROLOGUE

PRESENT DAY - LAKE MICHIGAN

Jaime's feet crunched over the gravel path that led to her rental cabin, smiling at the scent of woodsmoke that wafted from the chimney before her. The nights were cooling enough that curling up in front of the fireplace with a warm cup of tea sounded like the perfect end to the evening.

After Chris had cut out early on dinner with her boss and his wife, Jaime had declined a drink with her manager, hoping instead that Chris' headache had subsided and he would be up for a nightcap. She had been slightly perturbed when he left as it was a good opportunity to further her career, but as her boss' wife had also left early, Jaime hoped they would be forgiven.

The door to the comfortable log cabin was locked, and Jaime pushed the key inside the lock, turning the knob with a creak. She welcomed the warmth that rushed toward her as she pushed open the door before dropping the keys on the small table standing next to the door, where they landed with a clink that echoed through the darkness.

An echo that caused a flurry of motion in the dim light in front of the fireplace.

Jaime froze, feeling like an intruder in her own home, as her mouth dropped open and dread filled her stomach. The couple, who had been locked in a heated embrace on the couch, were springing away from each other and stared in her direction, the man's face cloaked with shock and guilt.

"What in the…" Jaime peered closer, wishing she was wrong in what she saw, but recognizing both figures immediately. "Chris? Sylvia?"

Her long-time, live-in boyfriend and… her boss's wife?

"I—ah, J-Jaime," stammered Chris.

Like he could hardly remember her name.

Smiling coyly, apparently unaffected by the interruption, Sylvia rose in a cloud of floral perfume and smoothed her dress, then padded barefoot past Jaime to the door and slipped through. Jaime glanced over her shoulder in time to see her boss's wife slip on sandals that rested just across the threshold. How had she missed them when she had unlocked the door?

Jaime turned back to Chris, who was struggling to fit his jeans back over his hips.

"Jaime, I—"

"Do not say anything," she said, the words crossing her tightly clasped lips which were nearly as paralyzed as her emotions.

Jaime knew disappointment, knew what it meant to lose everything. Only, when she had lost her parents in a boating accident while they were on vacation in the Caribbean during Jaime's first year in college, it had been an unpreventable tragedy, the result of an unexpected storm that no one could have survived.

This – this was altogether different. This was betrayal.

Chris, her college sweetheart, had never met her parents, but had helped her overcome the grief she had thought would devastate her forever, had given her hope for the future. Jaime had given all of her focus to her work and to her relationship with the man with whom she had thought she would spend the rest of her life.

And now this… this was unforgiveable.

She turned back toward where he was still standing, dressed, although rather haphazardly.

"I never meant—"

"How could you," she spat out, her anger overwhelming the distress that had immediately filled her.

"This is just a misunderstanding," he began, but she pointed a finger to the door.

"Get out."

He ignored her, rounding the woven couch that had provided the setting for his betrayal.

"You've just been so busy with work, and now here at this retreat, you and your boss were so focused on the account you were discussing, I felt invisible, you know? It's always work, or reminiscing about your parents, all the trips you took to Scotland. The land you want to go back to. I've been waiting for you to focus on *us*, and what *I* want. I just needed a break, and then Sylvia knocked on the door, and—"

"Get. Out. Now." She heard the deadness of her voice, knew her face was void of emotion as she stared him down. All she wanted was for him to leave, to get out of this cabin and out of her life — forever.

She walked over to the closet, forcing it open with superhuman strength as she began tearing his clothes off the hangers, taking great joy in flinging them haphazardly across the room and into his suitcase.

"But Jaime, where am I going to stay? This place is full and the next town is miles away. It's the middle of the night!"

"Why don't you ask Sylvia?" she snorted.

"Jaime—"

"I don't care where you stay. You are not my problem anymore."

Finished emptying the closet, Jaime sat on top of the stuffed suitcase, a grim smile crossing her face at the knowledge that all of the clothing he kept so meticulously ironed and folded would now be wrinkled and crumpled together. She zipped the suitcase, catching fabric as she did so, before opening the door to the cabin and throwing it outside. One blue shirtsleeve waved pathetically from where it caught in the zipper. She held the door open, looked at him, and said nothing.

Finally, he sighed, shook his head, and followed his bag out the door. He had barely made it across the threshold when she slammed the door after him.

Once he was gone, she sank to the floor, holding her head in her hands.

She knew what she should feel. Abandoned. Betrayed. Desolate.

But surprisingly, she also felt… free. She had thought for so long that Chris was her future, but really, was he holding her back in the past?

In that entire exchange, there was one thing he said that she focused on. Something that shouldn't matter, but she couldn't shake, that she held onto like a life raft.

There was only one place she felt at home, one place where it seemed that everything was right in the world.

Scotland.

Or, more precisely, the cottage in Crieff where her family still owned land – land that was hers now.

She'd lost Chris, and she couldn't see how she could face her boss again, knowing what she did about his wife. Her mother had always told her, "You only have one life, Jaime, so live it to the fullest."

Maybe it was time she started following that advice.

CHAPTER 1

PRESENT DAY - BOSTON, MASSACHUSETTS

The water beaded up on the plexiglass windows separating the travelers in the crowded airport from the planes waiting to take them to destinations around the world. Jaime stared out through the running droplets at the jets landing and departing on the runway. The clouds thickened and the wind feverishly blew the runway's bright red windsocks in all directions.

Jaime was lost in her thoughts as people boarded flights around her, the speakers from above calling out gate changes and boarding sections. She had made sure to get to the airport with more than enough time to spare. While the gate for her flight to chilly Scotland was fairly empty, when she had arrived at the ticket counter she had been surrounded by families and romantic couples in their beachwear heading for sunny destinations.

She sighed when her phone buzzed, knowing who it would be. Chris.

Hey. Where are you? I thought we were going to talk?

Jaime hadn't told him she was leaving. She had packed her keys, her passport, and a few items of clothing before leaving the apartment behind. All she had told Chris was that he had a week to find new accommodations. What she chose to do with her life no longer had anything to do with him.

Jaime took great satisfaction in switching her phone to airplane mode and tossing it into her purse. Why would he think there was anything left to say? Jaime returned to the window, catching her reflection. She looked terrible, but she knew it wasn't due to her mood over the break-up, but more so her uncertainty of her future.

Her long strawberry blonde hair was pulled back in a messy bun, her blunt cut bangs tickled her forehead, and her oversized sweater and yoga pants were at least ten years old. Sure, she had packed some nice clothes, but she figured jumping off a plane where it was, at the most, forty degrees, and riding a train from Edinburgh to Crieff called for comfortable and warm.

The loudspeaker crackled and cracked above her as an attendant stepped up behind the desk at her gate and turned on the phone. She typed on the computer for a minute before actually speaking. Jaime couldn't help but stare at her, feeling like there was something just a bit odd about the woman. Her hair was a flaming red with lipstick to match, thick-lensed glasses that she kept pushing up her nose every few seconds overwhelming her face. She looked, Jaime thought, confused and out of place more than anything.

"Abernathy. Jaime Abernathy. Would you please come to the front desk?" the woman's nasally voice called out.

Jaime sighed, figuring the nearly empty flight to Scotland was cancelled. That would be just her luck. She piled her purse on her carry-on and wheeled it up to the gate, where she stood for a moment, waiting for the woman to notice her. Eventually, Jaime cleared her throat, catching the woman's attention.

"I'm Jaime Abernathy." She waited for the woman to respond. "Please don't tell me this flight has been cancelled."

"Ticket?" the woman happily chirped, ignoring her complaint.

Jaime, who still preferred to hold a paper ticket opposed to trusting one on her phone, slid her ticket across the counter and watched while the woman, whose name tag read "Fiona," held it close to her face before beginning to type on the keyboard. Minutes later, she finally looked up at Jaime and smiled.

"You have been upgraded to first class. Here is your revised ticket. We board shortly," she said, a lilt to her voice.

Jaime stared at her, wondering if she had heard her wrong. "Really?" she said with disbelief. "There must be a mistake."

"Nope." Fiona smiled and leaned forward. "Broken hearts need better seats."

"I'm sorry, what did you say?" Jaime felt like she was in the twilight zone. How did this woman know she had a broken heart?

"You just seem like such a sad person," Fiona explained. "Thought I'd brighten your day!"

"Oh," Jaime laughed at herself, suddenly feeling rather self-conscious that she had been wearing her emotion far too plainly. "Thanks."

She lugged her bag back over to the chairs and plopped down, looking at the seat change on her ticket. Her turn of luck came as a surprise. Perhaps it was a sign she had made the right decision to travel to Scotland. She looked back up to the desk, but the woman had disappeared. Jaime shrugged her shoulders and shoved her jacket inside her carry-on. She rooted through her purse to make sure she had brought her tablet and headphones for her phone since it was almost a nine-hour flight from Boston to Edinburgh, and she could never sleep on planes.

After another few minutes, the plane began to load, and Jaime walked on board, happy to see her seat was near the front and at the window. She appreciated the luxury of having a few extra minutes to retrieve all of the essentials she would need to travel. She stowed her carry-on in the carriage overhead and plopped down in the cushioned seat, stretching her legs out in front of her in the glorious space. Much better than coach. An older gentleman sat next to her and smiled as he took off his large-brimmed hat and laid it on his lap.

I could get used to this.

Once the plane was finally in motion, Jaime leaned her head against the window and watched as the green field outside changed to empty gray sky while the engines rumbled around her.

The flight was smooth despite the dreary weather, and Jaime decided to have a few celebratory drinks. About three hours into the flight, against all the odds, Jaime was passed out, fluffy first-class blanket and all.

By the time she woke up, the plane was starting its descent, and she couldn't believe how quickly the time had passed until the alcohol-induced headache hit her hard and she downed the bottle of water she found resting in the seat-back basket in front of her.

Once the plane landed and pulled into the gate, the older gentlemen pulled her suitcase down from above and handed it to her. She smiled and wiped the side of her face, where it seemed she had laid her head in some cracker crumbs. As she passed the flight attendants on her way out, she noticed Fiona standing near the door smiling at her. Was it usual for the gate attendant to fly with the plane? She supposed some attendants had multiple duties.

"Enjoy the flight?" Fiona asked, as chipper as she had been hours ago.

"Yes, thank you so much for the upgrade," Jaime said with the happiest tone she could muster.

"Enjoy your stay in Scotland and make sure to *really* take in all that history," Fiona said, her ever-present smile following Jaime as she walked off the plane and into the tunnel leading to the terminal.

The bus to the train station was very easy to find, which took some stress off Jaime's shoulders since she had a tendency to get lost. It was only a few minutes ride and Jaime climbed onto the train and let the conductor punch her ticket. It would take about an hour to travel from Edinburgh to Crieff, so Jaime leaned back in her chair and watched the beautiful scenery fly by. It was just as she had remembered from her childhood, very green with small castle-like buildings and lush forests everywhere. The longer she traveled, the more the memories from her youth became brighter, steadier, warmer, and the relief she had felt at Chris' departure only increased at her return to the country that had long been her second home.

Between the train ride and the drive to her family's house, Jaime's spirits were lifted by the sheer beauty of the landscape around her. Her family's land was just five or six kilometers outside of the actual village of Crieff, but it felt worlds away from civilization, so she stopped her rental car at a small store for some groceries before continuing on. She made sure to both consult her map and confirm directions with the clerk behind the counter, and except for one questionable turn, she reached the cottage without much incident. By the time she was pulling up the drive to her family's home, the sun was starting to go down and jet lag was setting in.

Jaime stopped the car in the front drive, climbing out and retrieving her luggage before standing in the front yard, tilting her head back to look at the cottage. It was just as she had remembered from when she was here as a child. The last time she had visited, she would have been about fifteen, but the house still welcomed her with its jagged shingles, red shutters, and wooden arches that made it seem like it belonged in a fairytale. The structure was surrounded by lush greenery, with the hills of Scotland far in the background, creating a postcard picture, and a smile tugged at her lips.

She was happy to find her key worked with no issue as she let herself in. No one had stayed at the cottage in years, so she had hired a cleaning service to come the day before to prepare everything. It wasn't something she would normally do, but she wanted this time to be simple and relaxing. Fighting through cobwebs and doing laundry was the last thing she wanted to face when she arrived.

Jaime unloaded her groceries before plopping down on the overstuffed bed in the back bedroom. Perfect, she thought, laying her head down on the pillow. She was exhausted, but after a few minutes of rest, she forced herself off the bed to make some dinner.

The kitchen was set up just as she had remembered and Jaime stood for a moment looking around, recalling the last time she had been here. She could remember her mother's smile and laugh so perfectly. Her mom had been equally at home here, her red hair and green eyes vibrant against the Scottish landscape. That last trip was all laughter and exploring, and Jaime hoped she could leave here feeling the same way she did so many years ago.

For once accepting the memory and all the emotions that

came with it rather than pushing it away, Jaime wiped a small tear from her eye and walked over to the sliding door.

She looked out the glass pane at the patio set and decided it was the perfect night to bundle up and enjoy her dinner on the deck. She pulled out the steak, vegetables, and wine she'd purchased and then went to work making her meal. Jaime struggled to get the cork from the bottle but after a few grunts and choice words, she was taking a swig straight from it.

When her dinner was finally made, she sighed in contentment, gathered her plate and bottle of wine, and turned toward the patio doors. Rain had soaked the deck, leaving it sodden. How in the world had she missed the apparent typhoon that went through while she was cooking?

Shrugging her shoulders, Jaime left the door open a crack to let in the fresh, heady scent of rain-filled air, settling for a seat at the large dining table in the center of the cottage. The chatter of crickets and birds outside echoed through the house, and she was reminded how rustic this place was without television or radio. Jaime was determined to enjoy the silence and a good meal, and realized as she did so how long it had been since she had simply relished eating her food, without any distraction.

When she was done, she closed the door, grabbed her bottle of wine and plopped down on the floor in front of the fireplace. Chris had been the one to tend to the fire at the last cottage they had visited – well, that among other things – and the stacks of newspaper, old wood, and long matches set in front of the fireplace only served to confuse her. But after another swig of her wine, she started balling up the paper, replaying her father starting a campfire in her mind. Once the newspaper was shoved beneath a bedding of kindling, she struck a long match and set it on fire. Flames flickered then rose with more confidence, and she threw a few pieces of wood on top of the blaze and leaned back, triumphant.

Her victory lasted until the newspaper burned out and the wood hadn't caught fire.

Well, that was that. Jaime scowled at the dying embers, picked up her bottle of wine, and headed to the bedroom where she knew a soft bed and warm blankets awaited her. She unpacked her suitcase and threw on her plaid PJ pants and a button-up flannel before sitting down in the bed and pulling the covers up to her chest. She set the bottle of wine on the nightstand and inched down farther, rubbing her feet across the flannel sheets.

As the sun sank lower in the sky, Jaime snuggled into the warm down comforter and drifted off to sleep, leaving all the drama of the past month behind her, determined not to think of it while she was in her temporary home. Instead, she was finally ready to dive into her heritage and figure out why this place, of all places, was calling her name. It had been a rather uneventful day, but there must be more awaiting her. She couldn't explain how she knew that, but somewhere, out there, was her answer.

Jaime told herself before falling asleep that she would do some exploring the next morning. She was hoping to find whatever it was that she was looking for, and she thought a good walk through the woods, connecting back with nature, would be the perfect place to start.

CHAPTER 2

The bright sunshine beamed through the windows and straight onto Jaime's face. She groaned and smashed the extra pillow over her head, forgetting for a moment that she wasn't at home. The scent of the lavender laundry detergent on the sheets reminded her where she was, and she sat up straight in bed as excitement – something she hadn't felt in far too long – took over.

The second she threw the covers to the side, arctic air blasted her, and she shivered. If the air was this cold in the house, it must be freezing outside despite the rare Scottish sunshine. Jaime grabbed her slippers from her suitcase and shuffled into the kitchen, stopping to shake her fist at the fireplace, which stared back at her in silent victory.

She opened the fridge and grabbed a Danish from the package, started the coffee maker, and stood half-awake, staring out at the field behind the house. The hiss of the machine and the fragrant brew snapped her out of her trance and she poured herself a large cup, grabbed the quilt from the couch, and headed out to the deck. The morning air was crisp, and she stopped to throw the blanket over her shoulders before sitting down and taking a sip of her steaming black coffee. Jaime closed her eyes as the warm liquid flowed down her throat and heated her entire body. The sounds of birds chirping and the smell of nature calmed her nerves, enough to overcome the chill in the air.

Jaime's family owned several hundred acres, but when she was a child, her father had led her only so far during their explorations. Directly behind the house was what had once been a carefully landscaped area with a bonfire pit, some lounge chairs, and shrubbery, although most of it had been taken over by nature once more. Beyond that was a large field with tall waving grasses that led to the edge of the woods. The giant fir trees loomed in the distance, and the streams of light shining through the canopy were warm and inviting. Though leaf season was over, there was no more magical place on earth than the forests of Scotland.

After Jaime finished her makeshift breakfast, she shuffled back inside and grabbed her bag, looking for her toothbrush. She pulled her phone from the front pocket and clicked it on. Once it was on the home screen, it began to buzz loudly, notification after notification of text messages appearing on the screen. Most of the messages were from Chris; six of them, to be exact. They ranged from, "please talk to me," to "why can't we work this out," to the ever annoying, "I messed up, please forgive me." She clicked through each message, deleting as she went. When all messages were clear, she triumphantly nodded her head but then scowled as the phone buzzed in her hand.

When you've read this, call me. Let's talk.

Her groan of disgust accompanied a toss of the phone into the air. She was on her feet before it even hit the plank floor, and she walked away without a glance to where it landed. That was it — she needed to get out of the house and take in some nature. She slipped a pair of jeans, a Henley pullover, and a sweater from her suitcase and got dressed. She laced up her hiking boots up and pulled her hair into a tight ponytail.

In case of a hunger emergency, Jaime quickly packed a bag with fruit, a bottle of water, and a couple of Danishes because, hey, she was on vacation. She flipped the light switch off and headed out the back door, making sure to leave it unlocked since she'd left the keys inside and didn't feel like walking back past her phone again.

Once out in the fresh, crisp air again, Jaime instantly felt better. She took off toward the field and waded through the tall grasses that came up past her waist. She was just over five feet, but the reeds were higher than she remembered. As a child, she had always visited during the summer, when the fields had been covered in flowers. She could remember chasing her father through them, laughing and running as he tried to scare her. Then one day, they picked a ton of flowers and brought them back to her mother, who separated them into five different vases and placed them all over the house. Jaime's mom had loved flowers and, even in Massachusetts, their home had always been fragrant with fresh cut bouquets.

As Jaime made her way through the reeds to the tree line, she glanced back at the small cottage in the distance and was struck by a crazy wish to live here full time. Nothing was impossible, she supposed, but how could she make a living as a marketing analyst from here? Would she get lonely on her own after a time? Jaime turned back and started along the trail, thinking it was best she stayed in a familiar line of sight, her tendency to get lost high on her mind.

The sunlight streamed through the tree limbs and lit up

the forest bed. Birdsong filled the air, and Jaime paused as three small deer bolted from the path in front of her, not used to humans in their midst. The scene was like something out of a fairytale and Jaime half expected to see a gnome or sprite playing in the ferns on the edge of the trail.

The farther she walked into the woods, the more she became lost in the majesty of her surroundings. She decided to go continue her venture because, after all, she could always turn around and go back the way she came, if she just followed the meandering trail. The cold air brought her long-dormant senses to life, and the scurrying of furry animals made her feel the wonderment of a child. As she walked, Jaime looked up at the canopy above her, wondering what it would be like to jump from tree to tree. As she imagined her monkey antics, her head tilted toward the sky and she tripped over an object in her path and tumbled to the ground just beside the path.

"Ouch," she murmured as she rubbed at her knee, looking back to see it had been a log which had taken her down. How had she not seen it? Besides what seemed like a bruised knee, she was otherwise in one piece and she picked herself up, ruefully laughing. As she dusted off the front of her sweater, she decided it was time to return home and she turned around to take the well-worn path back.

Only... it wasn't there. That was odd. She could have sworn she was, at most, but steps away from it.

Jaime turned in circles trying to figure out how she'd gotten so far off the path. She tried to retrace her steps each way, but the ground was covered in wet leaves, and she couldn't find her footsteps to follow back to where she'd started. Not even one leaf appeared to have been disturbed. She glanced up at the sun, pursing her lips as she tried to remember from where in the sky it had beamed down on her, and walked in the other direction to try to find her way back to the field. Every tree looked familiar, but then, every tree also looked exactly the same.

Jaime's level of frustration shot from zero up to a thousand very quickly as she rounded the corner and tripped over the same log she had tripped on an hour before.

She was back where she had started and yet no closer to where she was trying to go. She hit her fist against the tree as she groaned in vexation, finally deciding to stop for a moment to collect her thoughts and gather her wits about her. She took her bag from her back and propped herself up against a tree, pulling out an apple and a bottle of water to rest for a bit as she attempted to come up with a plan that would get her back home.

Knowing her horrific sense of direction, she knew she should have stuck to her original plan and stayed within sight of the house. And if it wasn't for Chris and his damn texts, she would have her phone with her now and could GPS her way out of here.

Where's a gas station when I need one? She thought. She really didn't want to get eaten by some furry creature creeping around in the woods or... even more worrisome because it had a much greater chance of coming true, starving or freezing to death if she couldn't find her way out of here.

Unable to finish anything more than the apple with her stomach nervously flip-flopping, Jaime stood up and took a deep breath, ready to start again. She walked straight this time, only moving slightly to avoid running into a tree.

Step by step, she was sure she must be getting closer to the house, though she knew she hadn't been walking that long before she had tripped over the log.

Her heart pounded faster while her feet stepped slower as

the air grew cooler and the sun began its descent. Jaime forced herself to pick up her pace, even though fear was making her breathless and the day of walking had caused her legs to ache. The sound of creatures in the dark was setting her on edge. Fear overcame fatigue and she hastened her footsteps to where she was almost jogging through the trees. As the light started to fade, Jaime's nerves unleashed and she broke into nearly a full out sprint.

She weaved in and out of the trees. A sharp pain on her arm drew her to a stop. Frowning, she rubbed the scrape a looming limb had made. Tears filled her eyes and she peered through the dimming daylight. It was hard to see through the branches, and her despair bloomed through her chest. People died all the time from getting lost in the woods, and no matter how many adventures her parents took her on as a kid, Jaime lacked the knowledge to go full survivor mode in the Scottish forest.

"How could the path just disappear?" she muttered in between gasps.

There! From the edge, she saw the expanse of grass she had been searching for.

As relief flooded through her, she started running again, this time unaware of where she was stepping. As she reached the place where she expected to be surrounded by lush grass, she found nothing more than a clearing in the woods.

"Damn it!" she screamed to the trees. Why was nothing making sense?

Jaime bent down to catch her breath, fighting back the tears of panic stinging her eyes. The light was almost gone now, but she didn't want to stop yet. Striding fast, but not quite at a jog, Jaime moved through the woods searching for any sign of familiar surroundings. Something, anything that she had seen on the way into the forest.

As she stepped forward, expecting to feel the soft earth

beneath her feet, her body fell forward into the darkness. She shrieked in terror as she flailed her arms wildly around her. The wind rushed past her, and the sides of the dark hole began to move so quickly it looked like stars surrounding her. She fell faster and faster until her vision finally gave out and darkness overtook her.

CHAPTER 3

1544 ~ NEAR CRIEFF, SCOTLAND

The creaking sound of the cart's wheels echoed across the waving grassland outside of Crieff. The horse's hooves clapped slowly down the muddy path as the journey back to Perth began.

Alec McDermont, soon to be laird of the McDermont clan, had brought his brother along to sell their black sheep to the merchants at the Tryst. Crieff was known to be a town of thieves and drunks and even though Alec stood a head taller than most men, his shoulders nearly twice as broad, having another man with him seemed like a good idea. As they continued along the path, however, with Balloch complaining about every little thing, Alec was considering handing him over to the thieves for a bit of peace and quiet.

"I dinna understand why we didna press for that extra bag of barley," Balloch went on about the unfair trade of sheep. "How are the clans supposed to grow and prosper?"

"They are not supposed to, Balloch, that's the point," Alec groaned, already tired of the conversation.

"Well, what are they s'posed to be doing then?" Balloch asked.

"Look," Alec snapped, stopping the horse and turning to his brother. Balloch was tall and thin, with a habit of over-thinking everything. "Do ye really believe Mary Queen of Scots wants clans taking over? No. The royal stay royal and the farmers stay farmers, that's how 'tis."

"I dinna believe that is very fair," Balloch grumbled as he walked, and Alec decided the best course of action was to ignore him.

"We took too long in Crieff. We should go through the Pass and save us time," Alec decided as he walked forward.

"I think not — Crieff's Pass is where all the murderers and thieves lurk," Balloch responded with a shake in his voice.

"Good," Alec said with a firm nod of his head. "I'll hand ye over to them and have a quiet trip home."

"We canna simply take the main road?" Balloch pleaded.

"If we want to trade with these farmers for hides and still make it back to Perth we need to cut through the Pass, so stop complaining and move," Alec directed sternly.

The path through Crieff's Pass was no more than a worn-down lane through the woods. Early morning sunlight streamed in between the arching branches of the canopy of trees, creating a false sense of comfort for those traveling through. Alec walked slowly, his hand placed firmly on the handle of his sword while Balloch looked around him warily, as if there was someone waiting for him behind every tree and bush. The ground was wet from recent storms and ice clung to the shadowy patches of moss. It was unseasonably warm for Scotland in November as the ground normally would have a light covering of snow by this point. Even with the increased temperatures, however, the cold breeze still bit at Alec's bare upper body, only covered by the fur-lined cloak thrown over his shoulders.

The two men paused as several deer pranced across the path, stopping only for a moment to gaze at the unusual travelers, apparently sensing their lack of threat. Alec leaned over and pulled an apple from the cart and began eating it while walking, his eyes still roaming his surroundings. He had always been a cautious man, and unlike his brother, had grown up understanding he would one day become laird of the McDermont clan. This would be the last trip they would take to Crieff before the harsh winters buried them in, and it was imperative Alec protect their goods from thieves looking to score their next bounty.

It was already past midday, and though they would make it to the cattleman for trade with enough time, Alec knew they would need to camp out on the other side of the Pass before beginning their return journey to Perth. Alec's father had stayed home with Alec's sisters. It was the first time he had done so, and while he claimed Alec needed the experience, in truth, Alec felt that his father couldn't recover from the death of his wife, a tragedy if there ever was one. She had been found at the side of the road, apparently set upon by thieves, a supposition that was up for debate with Alec. All that had been stolen was her ring, the very one his father had given her on their wedding day years ago, after he'd taken her from his rival, Rory Gillie.

Alec's thoughts wavered from his current surroundings to his upcoming arranged marriage to the Gillie woman he despised and the clan he would rather see dead than attached to him by name. His father, fatigued in his grief, wanted peace, but Alec was sure the Gillies had ulterior motives.

Suddenly shaken from his thoughts when he sensed the change around them, Alec pulled the reins on the horse and stopped, shushing his brother before he spoke. As he sat listening to the tones fluctuating around him, searching for a sign of danger, he shifted slightly in his stance and waited for a response from the birds who just moments ago stopped singing. Across the landscape of forest, for the first time this trip, there was nothing but silence. No birds, no insects, and no falling acorns from a traveling squirrel could be heard.

He turned, ignoring the fearful look on Balloch's face, and searched the ground around them. There was no evidence that anyone was following them, and yet the immediate, unnatural silence of the forest kept him on edge. As Alec returned to his position next to the horses and readied himself to continue, a sound broke through the trees. The loud bang was followed by the snapping of limbs and ended with a thud on the ground.

Alec crouched down in reaction, turning his attention to the cloud of dust and leaves that had blown up in the air across the forest bed. He stood and stepped carefully toward what he realized with a shock seemed to be a body in the mud. With each step, he looked to both sides, half expecting to be bombarded by a group of thieves as they sprang their trap upon him. As he moved closer, the lump groaned in pain. He squinted his eyes in the dim light at the lump on the ground and saw the strawberry glimmer of flowing hair and the rosy cheeks of a lass lying motionless in the soil.

Still wary, he picked up his pace and slid down on his knees at her side. He searched the woods around him, not understanding where she had come from. There were a few twigs broken beside her, but no tracks to or from her in either direction. It was as if she had just... fallen from the sky.

The girl, who looked not much younger than he, was wearing what looked to Alec to be men's trews for the winter months and a very evenly knitted plaid on top. Her shoes were a strange, slick material that didn't look as if they had come from any cattle he had ever seen. Still, lying in the leaves, mud splashed on her freckled cheeks, she was a sight to see. Her beautiful skin was pale and soft, and the blonde specks in her hair almost glittered in the sunlight. Her freckles were like a map across her nose, and something in Alec longed to reach out and trace them with his finger. He sat staring at her for a moment when her eyes flew open without warning, revealing a striking shade of green irises, as she looked up at the sky but remained perfectly still.

"Lass?" Alec asked cautiously. "You seemed to have taken quite a fall."

"What?" The girl replied, her eyes darting toward Alec. "What happened? Where am I?"

"I am unsure where you are from, though not from around these parts with a voice like that," Alec said scratching his head. "But this is Crieff's Pass."

She sat up, still shaking slightly from her disorientation. Alec put his hand behind her in case she was to fall backward again. She looked down at her muddy boots and then around the landscape of trees. Her face showed pure confusion as she peered at the sun.

"Did I sleep here?" she asked, looking over at Alec, her eyes wild with panic and fright. "I remember losing the light and becoming so very lost. And then…."

"And then what happened?" Alec asked, trying to help her connect the pieces, as curious as she was by the outcome of her story. She was certainly striking, and Alec found himself leaning in closer toward her, wanting more from her… yet concerned that he might be taking advantage, for the woman clearly wasn't right in the head.

"I stepped in a hole, and I began to fall. I just kept falling and falling," she whispered to herself.

"Here let's get you on yer feet. You must have hit yer head

and had a fright," Alec said, putting his hands under her arms which were slim but strong, and lifting her up. She was a bit off balance and leaned into him, the scent of lavender filling his nose as strands of her soft hair brushed against the skin of his chest, bared through the cloak.

"Do you have a cell phone I can use? I could call my neighbor," the girl asked, still looking around her in confusion.

"A cell... phone?" Alec asked with curiosity, lifting a brow.

"Yes, a cell phone. Although you might not have room for one in that costume," she said, looking him up and down.

"I do not have this... cell phone."

She furrowed her brow as she stared at him incredulously. "It's the 21st century. Everyone has a cell phone."

"Twenty-first century?" Alec repeated, his brows furrowed. "What do you mean by this?"

"The time? The year?" she said, looking at him like he was daft.

"The year," he repeated her, wondering just how hard she had hit her head. "The year is 1544, lass."

"Fifteen... 1544?" the green-eyed girl said to herself as she eyed him up and down again, and he didn't miss the way her eyes lingered on his bare chest above his plaid. "What kind of weird game are you playing? Is this one of those role-playing things? A battle reenactment or something like that? My cousin used to do those, but it was more of a revolutionary war-type of thing. Although I suppose in Scotland—"

"Let us sit and you can drink," Alec said, firmly but with concern. "Do you belong to a clan? I'm Alec McDermont of Perth."

"Clan? I am Jaime Abernathy of ... well ... I don't really know anymore," she said with a bit of sadness in her voice. "Massachusetts, I suppose, although Crieff at the moment."

They walked back over to where Balloch was standing

and staring at the newcomer, this Jaime Abernathy, his eyes wide in wonder. She smiled at him and took the canteen of water Alec held out to her, running her other hand down the side of the horse. She passed the container back to Alec and put her hands on her hips, looking around her in confusion as though unsure of just where she should go or what she should do now. Alec tried not to stare as blatantly as Balloch, but her legs were a sight in the trews. He wanted to cover her with his spare plaid but didn't want to insult her.

"Ye must walk with us," Alec finally decided, looking up at the sky through the trees. "A lady is not safe in these woods. We are almost to the clearing where we will rest for the night."

Jaime bit her bottom lip for a moment before nodding her head at Alec, accepting the idea. He smiled at her, pleased to get moving again. Hopefully along the way, they would find someone who knew where she belonged. They walked along in silence for quite some time before reaching the edge of the woods.

One moment, Jaime was walking along next to him, silent in contemplation. He could tell she was thinking by the way her nose wrinkled, and her teeth scraped her lip. Every now and then she would mumble to herself, causing Alec and Balloch to exchange a glance of concern over her head.

The next moment, as soon as they reached the field beyond the forest, Jaime gasped and suddenly took off, running past him and out toward the wild grass as though something was chasing her. Alec was about to run after her to make sure she came to no harm, when she stopped as suddenly as she had started her run, turning around in circles as she brought her hands to hold her hair up high over her head, her face a mix of despair and bewilderment.

"What in heaven's name are ye doing?" Alec hollered out to her.

"The house, it was right here," she said looking back at him and pointing to an open field. "I'm sure of it."

Alec looked at Balloch, who shrugged his shoulders. He handed Alec the reins to the cart and walked over to him, leaning in close.

"The girl is daft," whispered Balloch. The two stared at Jaime, who had sat down in the tall grasses and was now rummaging through the strange bag she carried.

"We've made it through the pass and the main road is just ahead," Alec said in a low voice. "We canna afford to be late, but we also canna leave this girl in the middle of the woods. Take the road home, I'll help her find her way, and then I should be but a half-day behind you."

Balloch seemed a bit apprehensive, but finally turned to Alec with a sigh. "I say just leave her be, but then, ye've always been known to be swayed by a pretty face. Ye know this girl is daft."

"All the more reason she needs help," Alec said, ignoring Balloch's barb. His brother was right, but he couldn't help that he felt sorry for the girl, could sense that she was adrift, that she needed someone to guide her to wherever she needed to be.

He and Balloch clasped hands for a moment before Alec gave Balloch a big thump on the back. He lifted one of the saddlebags off of the horse and filled it with everything he and the lass might need for their journey before he sent Balloch on his way.

Alec waited until Balloch disappeared around the corner before he sat down in the grass beside Jaime, his arms around his knees while he refrained from saying anything. Instead, he just watched her. She pulled a pastry from her bag and began to eat it, that haunted look now etched on her face. There *was* something very strange about this girl, but at the same time, he couldn't seem to take his eyes off her. He glanced down at her small, fragile hands and saw she didn't wear a ring, which meant she didn't belong to a man.

He sighed as the thought reminded him of his own upcoming nuptials, the very ones he was trying so hard to avoid. He should have found a wife for himself in Crieff along with supplies for the winter, he thought with a snort. It was the only way to avoid the one chosen for him. What was his new bride and her clan going to think when he arrived with a woman in tow, even if she was as daft as Balloch assumed her to be?

And then, as he sat in the blowing grasses next to this woman who had no idea where she came from or how to get home, a wild idea came to him.

The knock to her head seemed to have taken away Jaime's memory. He didn't know how long it would take her to get it back, but perhaps it would be just the right amount of time – time enough to sort through his dilemma with the Gillies.

He looked over, catching her wide-eyed stare, wondering if, perhaps, she could be his saving grace; an angel fallen from Crieff's Pass.

CHAPTER 4

*J*aime had pulled out the Danish for comfort, but once she sunk her teeth into it, she realized just how hungry she actually was. She chewed the sweet treat and looked out at the field where her family home had once stood… or would, apparently, one day stand.

Was the man beside her right? Had she hit her head so hard that she was creating some wild, fantastical dream?

She had been sure that he was jesting with her, that he must be so deep into his character that he refused to be rational. But then when they reached the clearing… this time, Jaime knew that she was in the right place, that this was her family's land, where the cottage should be standing.

But here she was, sitting in an empty field where the living room should be.

So did she, in fact, travel through time, or had she finally lost her mind?

All those years after her parents died, people watched and waited for her to finally crack, and now, it had actually happened. Her mind had left her lost in a familiar place but in an unfamiliar time.

Jaime distracted herself from her rather unhelpful thoughts by taking a moment to truly study the man next to her. He was tall and broad, the crest of a well-developed chest muscle peeking out through the cloak wrapped around his shoulders. Beneath it, he was wearing a plaid type of blanket around his waist which then looped over his shoulder. He looked like he was straight from Outlander.

Outlander. In which Claire travels through time back to Scotland.

Jaime let out a groan and smacked the heel of her hand against her forehead. She had binged the series about a month ago. Obviously her mind was playing tricks on her, casting her into one of her favorite shows.

And now, studying this man, she knew she had to be dreaming. For he was simply too fascinating to be real. He was tall and muscular, and she had a strange urge to reach out and run her hands over the ab muscles that peeked out of his cloak. He wore his auburn hair long and it drifted over his forehead to frame his handsome, chiseled face. His cloak looked cumbersome but warm, which Jaime assumed was necessary since the blanket-garment was like a skirt covering the lower half of his body, with only his boots below it.

He *seemed* genuine, and she couldn't believe he was part of a practical joke being played on her, but she had to test him.

"Alec," Jaime began. "If this is 16th century Scotland, who is the King?"

"We dinna 'ave a King," he replied, looking out at the horizon.

"Every country has a leader," she retorted, pointing her finger at him.

"Aye," he said, slowly turning toward her. "We have a Queen. Mary Queen of Scots, who took the throne only two years ago."

"Oh," Jaime responded, slinking back down in disappointment, feeling foolish. Apparently, she needed to brush up on her Scottish history. She had heard of Mary Queen of Scots, but had no idea of when she reigned. "Tell me what you think."

Jaime grabbed her bag and dumped the contents out into a pile. He leaned toward her, the musky, masculine scent of him nearly overwhelming her as he eyed her warily before she started handing him items, one after another, watching his reaction. First was a pen, then a compact of makeup, a toothbrush, a credit card, a charger cord for the phone that was lying on the floor in this very spot apparently centuries away, and finally a brush. When the brush hit his hands, his eyes lit up, but before he could say anything, she rolled her eyes and grabbed the items back. Of course, he knew what a hairbrush was.

"Nothing is familiar – besides the brush?" she asked, and he shook his head slowly.

"Nothing."

"We're close to town," he said, standing and holding out a hand. "We should stop in, see if anyone recognizes you. If not, we can pick up a few supplies for you."

"That's perfect," Jaime said, a wide smile breaking out on her face. That's exactly what she needed – to be reacquainted with civilization, to remind herself of who she was, where she was, and when she was.

Jaime jumped up and started out into a quick pace toward the road that should be leading to her family's house. From behind her, Alec called for her to slow, and when she finally did, he reached her, his big hands settling on her upper arms before he turned her slightly left in a different direction. They trudged along together up the slight rise in the landscape, and when they reached the top, Jaime's heart leapt at what she knew would be before her.

"All right, modern world," she murmured. "Show yourself."

"Modern?" Alec repeated, and she jumped at his voice, low and warm in her ear. She hadn't realized just how close he was behind her.

"Yes, right—"

She stretched out a hand, but the words died in her throat when she looked out at the scene beyond, where the town was tucked in the distance. Her hands fell to her side at the sight in front of her.

People were walking the dirt road into the town, dressed just like the man beside her – and if they weren't walking, they were riding horses or pulling carriages.

"Well, hell." She said, raising her arms to cross them over her head as she began to pace back and forth. This was not a practical joke. She was either trapped in her own imagining that was something between a dream and a nightmare, or she actually had traveled through time.

She wasn't sure which she preferred to believe.

Suddenly the weight of the day, the length of time she had been walking, searching, fell over her, and she dropped to the ground, exhaustion settling upon her shoulders.

"Here, lass," Alec said, not unkindly, as he kneeled down next to her. "Let us go into town, get you some… female clothing. Then tomorrow we will head for my home right outside of Perth. It will take only a day and a half."

"Well," Jaime replied, considering her options, her head on her knees as she tried to acclimatize herself to all that was happening around her. He must think her a raving lunatic and yet here he was, helping her for no apparent reason but a kind heart. She could either go along with his plan until she could figure out what to do or sit here in her "weird clothes" and wait for a Scottish thief to drag her off. "Thank you, Alec, I do appreciate you taking the time to help me. But as soon as I figure out how to get back home – in whatever way that might be – I'll be leaving."

"Agreed," Alec responded as he stood up and reached one meaty palm down to help her up.

Jaime sighed and took his offered assistance, gasping at first at the contact of his warm hand despite the chill in the air, and then how quickly and effortlessly Alec lifted her to her feet. She threw her bag on her back and followed him down the hill and toward the town. As they approached the buildings, people in shop doors and those on the road stopped and stared at Jaime, whispering to each other in shock. She looked down at her clothes which were so terribly out of place and fidgeted uncomfortably.

Alec stopped in front of a small, nondescript wooden building which stood among rows of others just like it. Jaime held back a smile as the huge man in front of her tromped up the steps, nodding a greeting at the giggling ladies on the front porch. Inside there were several dresses hung up for display, the shop apparently belonging to a seamstress. Jaime ran her hand over the smooth material of a dress to keep her fingers busy as Alec spoke to the shop owner.

His voice, low and honeyed, drifted over to her, so in contrast to the tone of the seamstress. The woman's voice was nasally, loud, and… familiar.

Jaime whirled around, her eyes coming to rest on the woman next to Alec.

"I believe I have just the thing to fit her perfectly," the woman said, her red lips turning up into a smile as she stared knowingly at Jaime from across the room.

"Jaime," Alec called out. "This is Fiona. She will take care of yer attire. I will be waiting outside."

For a moment, Jaime just stood and stared at the woman with bright red hair and round glasses that were much more ancient now, convinced now that her mind had betrayed her, pulling together all of the pieces of her life and sending her into a world where they existed together. Fiona smiled at her and reached out her hand, waiting for Jaime to step forward. Alec, who had paused near the doorway, cleared his throat to get her attention, snapping Jaime back into reality. She reluctantly followed Fiona to the back of the building and stood, silent and stunned, while the seamstress pulled several garments from a large wooden chest.

"These will fit like they were made for you," Fiona said, apparently unaffected by the entirety of the situation.

"Have we… met before?" Jaime asked in a daze, as she reached out numb hands and took the clothing from Fiona.

"I dinna believe so, but this area is steeped in history," Fiona said cheerily. "Perhaps you have met one of me relatives. Now, go behind that dressing board and try everything on."

Jaime nodded as she took small steps forward, unable to tear her eyes from the familiar face of the flight attendant. Could resemblance remain that strong over four hundred years of generations? Jaime walked behind the partition and sorted the clothes out on the table provided. Luckily, she had dressed in similar clothing for Halloween several years ago and knew exactly what every piece was. She wriggled and grunted as she pulled, tied, and laced herself into the undergarments, dress, and wrap. When she was done, she stepped out from behind the partition and smiled awkwardly, wishing there was a mirror within so that she could see what she looked like dressed as a Highlander lass.

"Perfect!" the woman said with her thick Scottish accent, clapping her hands in delight. "This wrap will keep you very warm on yer journey, and those boots will be perfect for walking to Perth."

Jaime looked down at the leather boots she had shoved onto her feet and struggled to lace due to the uncomfortable layers of clothing. She wiggled her toes, realizing that they were nothing more than really thick leather booties, but thanked the woman as she collected her things, shoving them into her bag. She followed Fiona down the corridor and to the front of the shop, where she was pleasantly surprised to find a small, round mirror affixed to the wall. It was nothing like the full-length mirror in her bedroom at home and the reflection was smoky and yellow, but she could, at least, see that she was still herself. That much hadn't changed. Fiona pulled the hair tie out of Jaime's hair before brushing through the knots. She left her hair down and around her shoulders, passed her back the elastic band with no comment on its strangeness, then showed her out onto the porch.

Jaime stood at the top of the stairs watching Alec, whose back was to them until Fiona cleared her throat to get his attention. Jaime's cheeks warmed when Alec turned, for his face quickly transformed from one of impatience to one of shock.

Jaime looked down rather self-consciously at her dress, which was made of a dark green linen material that was tight at the top, with a scoop neck and long sleeves. It flowed to her waist, where mountains of fabric cascaded down to the ground. Her shawl reflected the dark green and red patterns of Alec's plaid, although it was made from the same thick material as her gown.

"I matched yer shawl to yer husband's clan colors," Fiona stated as Alec walked up to the two women.

Jaime's eyes shot toward Alec at the mention of their assumed matrimony, and Alec stepped forward and handed the woman some coins. She smiled at them and nodded before pocketing them as she turned and then walked back into the store. Alec put his hand out to help Jaime down the stairs, which she was more than happy to accept since she knew at some point this fabric was going to send her tripping to the ground.

She took one look back at the shop, seeing Fiona standing in the doorway, watching them. Just before she entered the store, she grinned and winked at Jaime, who stood staring after her until Alec's voice recaptured her attention.

"Yer a woman traveling alone with a man," Alec explained quietly as they passed others in the street. "So, for now, yer my wife. Understand?"

"Yes," Jaime said, deciding not to contest it and surprising herself when she was not at all disturbed by the thought.

"The sun has disappeared, so we will stay in the town for the night. I was able to secure our lodging, but we will have to share a room if we are to keep up this pretense," Alec continued.

"All right," Jaime said somewhat warily, clutching her bag to her chest as she wondered just what Alec might expect from their bed-sharing. She was not completely averse to the thought of getting to know him better, but she wasn't sure she was quite ready to jump into bed with him considering the fact that either her mind had turned on her or she truly was in the sixteenth century.

"Not to worry, lass," Alec said, apparently reading her mind. "I'll sleep on the floor. I wouldna dream of compromising your virtue."

Jaime scowled at what sounded like sarcasm, but then couldn't help the snort that emerged at what she realized was likely an attempt at humor. She followed Alec to another building, one in the same style as the rest but slightly larger. Alec spoke to the man in the front of the building and then led Jaime up the stairs and to a large bedroom at the end of the hall. Jaime paused in the doorway, taking it all in. The bed was stuffed with what looked like... straw? And draped with large fur coverings. The fireplace was already lit, and a large white fur rug was laid in front of it. On the table below the window was a thick candle, lit to break through the approaching darkness.

"The innkeeper said there would be cheese and bread," Alec said, nudging his chin toward the table as he took off his cloak and sat down before the fire. "We have a long trip so I figured ye should eat and we could get some sleep."

Jaime nodded and set her bag down on the floor next to the bed. She sat on the edge of one of the hard wooden chairs and picked at the bread and cheese, feeling oddly self-conscious at falling into such an intimate routine with a man she didn't know. She picked up the plate and crossed to the fireplace, which was drawing her as much as the man who sat in front of it.

"Here," she said, and he took the plate from her, his fingers brushing overtop of hers and she quickly backed away as though she had been burned. Where was a man like this, as handsome as he was kind, in her actual life? Apparently, the only way she could find a man like him was to conjure up one in her dreams.

She sighed as she shrugged out of her shawl and hung it over the back of one of the chairs. Unsure of protocol, she kept her dress on but slipped her boots off and left them by the edge of the bed. Alec had placed his cloak over the rug and was stretched out on top of it, eyes already closed. Jaime lay down on the bed and pulled the thick blankets over her, her dress giving her extra cushion, which she needed as the mattress was far from the soft down she was used to. She couldn't help staring over at Alec, whose face was flashing in the firelight.

Somehow, from the tenseness in the air, Jaime knew that he wasn't sleeping.

"Alec," she said in a stage whisper, "are you awake?"

"I am now," he said drolly.

Jaime paused, needing the connection to him but unsure how to break the awkward silence.

"Do you have a big family?" she asked, not sure how he would react to her curiosity.

"Wouldna call it big," he responded, his eyes still closed. "My mother died when I was young, and my stepmother a couple years ago, but I have a brother, the one you met on the road, two sisters, and of course my father."

"You aren't married?" Jaime asked before realizing her question might be rude.

"Not yet. My father has arranged a marriage, but I am… not exactly about it," he gruffed. "She is from a clan that has been at war with the McDermonts for many years. The marriage is supposed to bring peace between the clans but will bring none to my life."

"I see," Jaime replied, unsure of what to say at the thought of marrying a person chosen by another. "Is she a nice person?"

"Hardly," he scoffed, his eyes blinking open at the thought. "Alexandra Gillie. Part of the family, the Gillie clan, who I am certain enough had something to do with my stepmother's death." His gaze darkened. "I have only to prove it, as I've said nothing to my father, for I want to be certain first. I know Alexandra is the last woman on this earth I would want to tie myself to, for she does nothing but remind everyone how much better she is than the rest of us. The thought of giving her the McDermont name sets my stomach to ache."

"I'm sorry," Jaime replied, thinking of her most recent breakup. "I almost married once, but I broke it off with him after finding him in bed — well, on the couch — with my employer's wife. Which is what brought me here. I took a vacation to Scotland to get away from it all."

"Yer mate had relations with a married woman?" Alec asked, shocked. "Did they put her in the stocks?"

"No," Jaime laughed, enjoying the image of Sylvia losing that smug grin when she learned of such a punishment. "But I suppose that would have been fitting. In the end, I was more embarrassed than anyone."

"You shouldna be," he responded, more fierceness in his voice than she would have expected. "Yer a fine woman, a little strange after the knock to yer head, but mannerly, bonnie, and though short, ye have hips to bear a healthy brood."

"Ah…" Jaime searched for the right response, sensing that laughing at his words would only insult him. "I suppose you mean that as a compliment? In my time, 'brood-bearing hips' isn't really a requirement for a mate, nor something most women would want to hear."

"No matter," Alec responded, waving away her words. "The fault's on the two of them. Your clan should be grateful to be rid of him."

"I agree," Jaime said nodding her head. "Though my clan is pretty much just me now. My parents died several years ago and I have no siblings."

"I am sorry, lass," he responded with genuine empathy in his voice. "'Tis hard to lose a parent."

"It is," Jaime said, her thoughts floating off to her mom and dad.

"Well, Jaime from the future," Alec said after a few minutes of silence. "Have a good kip. We'll head out at first light."

Jaime had no idea what a kip was, but she assumed it was some kind of sleep. Hopefully in the morning, she would wake up to her true life and all would be fine. Maybe she would be lying in a hospital somewhere, coming out of a coma or some fever-induced dream. If only Alec, or a man like him, could be there waiting for her on the other side.

Of course, she said none of that to him. She simply wished him goodnight.

"Sweet dreams, Alec from the past."

Jaime rolled over to the rustle of the straw beneath her and stared out at the night sky through the window. The stars were so bright without the noise and traffic. She still wasn't sure if she believed what was going on was real, but she knew, for now, she was in safe hands, whether she had imagined them or not.

A night alone with this fine-looking man was something she would normally be grateful for rather than fearful of. She shook her head at herself and her thoughts as she closed her eyes and fell asleep listening to the crackling of the fire and the deep breathing of Alec McDermont, fast asleep on the sheepskin rug.

CHAPTER 5

Alec was awake before the sun had breached the horizon and walked as lightly as he could to the door to fetch some raw cheese and berries to break their fast. He looked back at Jaime, still sleeping soundly, the freckles on her nose bright from yesterday's sun, and ignored the tingle he felt in the pit of his stomach and the yearn to join the beautiful sleeping woman in the bed. He longed to do nothing but hold her until that furrow on her brow was eased, to stroke the softness of her hair as it fanned out behind her on the pillow.

Of course, he fought that urge, suppressing it deep within him as he let himself out of the room and tread down the stairs to the ground floor of the inn.

He emerged into the morning light, pulling his cloak around him as the November air hit him in the bare chest. The merchants were already out, and he was able to quickly find some food to take back up to the room, as he was urgent to return.

When he passed back through the doors, he nodded at the owner standing in the doorway of the building. The stairs were creaky, and Alec had a hard time staying quiet. As he entered the room, Jaime sat up and turned over in the bed toward him, her hair a red cloud around her, but she smiled at him through sleepy, though still somewhat confused, eyes.

He smiled back and set the food down on the table before walking over and smoothing her messy locks down, taking his time as he coiled one curl around his finger, releasing it to bob around her head. She blushed slightly and turned her eyes from his to the floor. Alec couldn't help but notice just how beautiful she was, especially now that she had rested and no longer looked quite as bewildered as she had yesterday.

"After we eat we will depart," Alec said, shaking the smile and warm glow from his face. "I would like to get as close as we can to home before we camp tonight. I took some blankets from the carriage before my brother left so we can sleep out."

"I like camping," Jaime smiled as she popped a berry into her mouth. "My parents used to take me all the time."

"Camping? You mean like making an overnight encampment when traveling?" Alec asked, scrunching his nose in Jaime's direction, unable to tear his gaze away or control his response as he watched her lick the juice of the berries from her lips.

She paused, her eyes wide, as he couldn't stop himself from reaching out to wipe her lip with his thumb.

"Oh, um, yes, except you do it for fun," she finally responded. "You build a fire – well, someone else does, as I'm wretched at it – and eat s'mores and tell ghost stories." She gave a half shrug. "At least that's what we did."

"What is a ... shmooore?" Alec's brow creased. "'Tis some kind of animal?"

"No." Jaime laughed, and he enjoyed the view of her perfect, even white teeth. "It's ... um... it's a dessert. Made of what we call marshmallows and chocolate and graham crackers. Nothing that you would have, except maybe some of the honey? You eat it."

"And ye do all of this for enjoyment?" Alec asked, not understanding why a person would choose to leave a building to sleep outside without a reason.

"Yes. We don't get out into nature a lot, so we do that for fun," she replied.

"The future sounds miserable," Alec said with a raised eyebrow and gave her a slight grin. He knew Jaime had done nothing more than take a hard knock to the head, but he liked seeing her smile, and so he humored her.

They finished their breakfast, gathered their things, and set out for Perth. The walk would be long but Jaime must have been feeling more comfortable with him, for she started talking about where she was from – or the world she had imagined. Alec listened intently, enjoying the strange lilt of her voice and laughed at some of her tales.

Alec thought she was fascinating, and even if she was half-mad, she had a wild spirit about her that called to him. Her stories reminded him of the tales his mother would tell late at night in the winter by the fire. As a child, he would imagine great wars and valiant battles against the English, who, according to Jaime, had reconciled with his people in her future, although he noticed the bit of unease that crossed her face when he asked about the centuries between them. Her skin glowed in the sunlight, and together her beauty and spirit captivated him as no other woman had before. He kept stealing glances at her, desire and something else he couldn't quite name pulling at him.

The day wore on, and they stopped twice to eat some of the bread and berries he had packed for the journey. Once the sun had started to set, Alec noted the drag in Jaime's step and the way her head began to bob lower as she hunched somewhat. He realized he had been so caught up in their destination and her stories that he had missed the exhaustion setting into her body, and began to look for a place to rest for the night.

He had to admire her. Jaime had not once complained, though she had commented on "the ridiculous extra fifty pounds of clothing" she was wearing. He looked at his surroundings and led her into the woods for some coverage from any danger lurking down the trail toward his home. They found a clearing and created a space for a fire. As Jaime laid out the blankets, Alec worked hard at starting a fire within the wet soil of the woods.

"Here," Jaime said reaching into her bag. "I actually have something that will help with a fire."

She held up a brightly colored red cylinder and smiled. Alec stepped forward and stared cautiously at it. She snapped her thumb over the small silver wheel, and a flame emerged, causing him to jump back with a hiss. Apparently realizing she had startled him, she let the tab go, extinguishing the fire.

"You have magic?" Alec said, cautious of the strange instrument that Jaime had brought to him. HE wasn't usually one to believe in such things, but…

"No," she replied stepping toward him, reaching out with the cylinder resting in the palm of her hand. "It's called a lighter. It makes a spark and creates fire."

"A very strange tool," Alec said turning back toward the stack of wood. He wasn't sure where she would have found such a contraption, but he decided it was better not to ask more questions. "'Tis not natural."

"Suit yourself," she said, tossing it back in her bag.

Once the fire was going, without the help of the contraption she called a "lighter," Alec sat down next to Jaime on the blanket and warmed his hands. An owl hooted in the distance, and she startled and moved closer to Alec. He could still smell the lavender in her hair as she hummed a strange tune he never heard. He smiled slightly, sensing her unease and enjoying the fact she was seeking comfort from him, and wrapped an arm around her shoulders. He turned and caught her face looking up at his, her green eyes flashing. She stared back up at him, seeming just as entranced by his face.

"Are ye warm enough?" he asked gently, his fingers unconsciously stroking her shoulder.

Jaime nodded her head, which was still tilted up toward him, and Alec turned his face away to fight his sudden urge to lean down and kiss her. It would not be right for him to take advantage of a woman in her current state. He could feel her shoulders slump slightly in response and he pulled his arm back as she sat up and reached her hand out to tip his face toward her.

"We should go to sleep," he murmured, his lips nearly touching hers.

"We should," she responded breathily, but instead of pulling away, she only leaned in closer. Alec was helpless to do anything but allow her soft, cold fingers to guide him, and as he turned, she pressed her warm lips against his.

He knew he should likely retreat, but she was so captivating, so alluring, that instead he drew her closer, as if to drink in all she offered him. Her lips moved over his and he couldn't help but respond, emboldened when she let out a slight moan as he leaned into her, his hand wrapping around her head, his fingers twisting into the red-gold silk of her hair.

She tilted her head back and he feasted on her, sliding his tongue into her mouth when her lips parted, inviting him in.

Alec wrapped his other arm around her waist, using it to gently settle her back on his cloak, which was spread on the ground beneath them. While she may have lain beneath him, Jaime was far from passive. Whether it was the night air or the heady magic that shimmered between them under the stars or a spell that she has cast over them, Alec let go of his conscious state of guard and ran his hands over her, unable to get enough.

He caressed her soft cheek, the bodice of her gown, the curve of her breast, her waist, until he could no longer settle for feeling her curves through the fabric, but needed more. He let his hands run down Jaime's back, his fingers finding the laces of her dress and slowly loosening them. He waited for her to pull back, leaned away from her to give her the opportunity to do so, but was pleased when instead she placed a hand on his chest, pushing him up and back as she rose onto her knees and ran her fingers through his hair, holding him close as she worshipped his mouth.

The sounds of the woodland creatures faded into the background as Alec's heartbeat, mixed with the sounds of Jaime's increased breathing, echoed through his ears. She was bolder than any woman he had ever known, and her hands over his hot skin excited him. He slid her dress down, off her shoulders, and she wriggled the rest of the way out. Slowly he untied her undergarments and slipped them from her body, kissing the skin they exposed. They both paused for a moment in sudden acknowledgement of what they were doing as they knelt, staring into each other's eyes, exploring one another with fingers, at first tentatively, but then slowly growing more eager and emboldened.

Her light skin glistened in the night, and he grabbed her by the waist, lowering her back down onto his cloak beneath them. Jaime's hands were as exploratory as his, running over his muscles, pausing here and there to circle a scar or two, left behind as memories of skirmishes between clans.

Alec couldn't help the groan that emerged as she slid her hands up his thighs, under his kilt, and then finally, without any hesitation, grasped his pulsating manhood. He grabbed her hand, for if she went any further, this would be over and done with before they even began.

Instead he reached down to ready her with his fingers, only to find that she was already more than eager to receive him. He dipped his head and took one rosy tip of her breast in his mouth, taking his time to worship it properly before moving over to the next.

She let out a moan as she arched up toward him, her hips inviting him to take her – an invitation he found he didn't have within him to turn down.

He positioned himself at her entrance, and as the red-tailed fox screeched through the night and the cold wind blew, Alec took Jaime next to the roaring and crackling of the fire. Their moans of ecstasy drowned out the surrounding creatures, and the warmth they created in the cocoon of the cloak and blanket caressed their naked bodies. Their passion for one another escalated until Alec was left holding on to Jaime, who shook in pleasure beneath him. He lowered himself down, yanking the blankets overtop of them and rubbed his cheek against hers, listening to her heightened breathing.

Jaime's grip on his back slowly lessened until all the muscles in her body were relaxed and she moved to her side as Alec lay next to her. She put her head on his heaving chest, and he watched as this strange creature fell asleep to the lullaby of his beating heart. Shortly after, he also fell victim to the comforting feeling of Jaime's warm touch and drifted off to sleep.

CHAPTER 6

Alec blinked as the sun filtered through his closed eyelids, and before he did anything, his lips began to curl into a slow smile as the previous night came rushing back through his memory.

He stretched an arm out, reaching for Jaime, but instead found an empty space where she had slept. He finally opened his eyes and turned toward the smoldering ashes of the fire, only to find her folding blankets and returning their things to the two bags they had brought with them. She looked up from beneath her lashes with pink cheeks and a small, hesitant smile.

"Good morning," she whispered.

"Mornin'," he replied, still watching her tidy up their makeshift campsite. "How did ye sleep, lass?"

"Just fine," she said shyly. "Although I can't say I've ever heard a man snore so loudly in all my life."

He laughed at that, a loud chuckle that washed away some of the tension that floated through the air between them.

"You've got something of a snore yerself," he retorted, and her eyes widened in indignation.

"I do not!"

"Pretty sure the woodlands creatures across the ocean stayed awake for yer snorin'," Alec teased as he stood up and pulled his plaid off the ground before tying it back around his waist.

Jaime had opened her mouth to respond, but the words seem to stick in her throat at the sight of him dressing. Alec grinned, happy to see her respond in something other than concern, enjoying the playful banter between them.

He helped her tidy the site, reaching out and touching her now and again, unable to resist his desire to keep her close. Eventually, they reluctantly pulled on their bags, eating oatcakes while they walked.

"We shall be there shortly," Alec said looking ahead at the horizon after a couple of hours. "Everything is lookin' familiar to me again."

"I hope that I won't be an inconvenience to your family," Jaime replied somewhat sheepishly, and he placed a finger underneath her chin, encouraging her to lift it high and not doubt herself. "I'll do whatever you need me to around the house."

"Trust me, yer going to be doing a great deal for my clan simply by being there with me," Alec responded as he continued to walk, until he realized that she had stopped somewhere behind him.

He glanced back nonchalantly and saw the look of confusion on her face. A trickle of guilt raced through him for tricking her, especially after all that had occurred between them last night, but he had to save his clan. Jaime falling from the tree to his feet was, to Alec, a sign, and one he was not going to ignore.

Alec reached back, taking her hand as he picked up the pace, hoping to have the introductions over with as soon as possible. He had a feeling that Jaime would get on well with his sisters, and once she understood what he was fighting to save, she would – hopefully – forgive him.

Alec could hear the crunching of the gravel as Jaime sped up to walk next to him. The cold air blowing across their path smelled of cinder and ash, telling Alec they were nearing the farm. His clan consisted of sheepherders, among other things, and it was just the right temperature for his father to demand a fire after working outside all morning. The cropping was over for the season, but the sheep they didn't sell this year would have to be sheltered and cared for through the cold months. They would also provide the wool his sisters and the women of the clan needed to make clothing and blankets. As they approached the top of the rolling hill, Alec stopped and sighed in contentment.

"There it is," he stated, looking out at his farm, the chimney of the rather large house billowing smoke from the fireplace. "Home."

"Wow," Jaime responded, the awe in her voice. "It's beautiful. It looks like a small castle."

"My grandfather's grandfather built it with his own two hands," Alec couldn't help but boast. "The McDermont clan started as poor farmers, and we have built our wealth and stature. There is no clan in Scotland that dinna ken our name by now."

"I remember touring old castles like this when I was a child," Jaime murmured. "It was always so enchanting, like a fairytale."

Alec's brow furrowed, as he looked down at Jaime as she spoke. He had nearly forgotten that she still fancied herself from a future century. Alec wished she would remember her true background, so he would have some sense of where she belonged, would know who she was and what she was dealing with. He knew if she spoke of this in the house, his father would have her thrown out as a madwoman – especially if Alec claimed her to be his bride. He took a deep breath and turned to Jaime.

"Things willna be as simple inside those walls as they have been on this journey," Alec stated firmly. "My father and sisters, they will nae understand what yer saying of how you came to be here. I must ask that ye don't speak of it in the house."

"Oh," Jaime said, her expression growing distant as though she were mulling the statement over in her head. "I understand, but what shall I say?"

Alec scratched his head. "Yer not from around here, that much is for certain. They will think ye to be English, which you likely are, lass. You must *not* let them think yer aligned with King Edward's way of thinking."

Jaime nodded. "Easy enough," she said resolutely. "And what am I doing here?"

He pretended not to hear her as they started down the hill. He knew he should tell her what his plan was, but he was too afraid that she would argue it, and then it would all be for naught. He'd explain himself later instead, he reasoned as he led her toward the farm, Alec's step lightening, speeding up as they approached. As they walked up the dirt road toward the towering stone home, Alec spotted his sisters peering out the window, glee on their faces before they left the window and opened the door, chattering excitedly. He dropped his bag as the youngest of the two left her post and sprinted out of the castle and into Alec's arms.

"Oh me wee darlin'," Alec said as he squeezed his sister, who was in her tenth year. "I missed you!"

Alec set her down on the ground and smiled as her wild hair, matching his color, blew with the wind. Her velvet green dress showed stains at the bottom, signifying she had been out in the fields that morning with their father. She turned to Jaime and smiled sweetly.

"Hello, there," Jaime said with a smile for his sister.

"Hilda, this is Jaime. Jaime this is Hilda, my tiniest of sisters," Alec stated, looking up at Jaime, unable to help the glow of pride for his sister.

"It's lovely to meet you," Jaime stated, shaking the little girl's hand.

"And you," she replied with a confused look on her face. "That is a strange accent ye have."

"She has traveled all over the world, so her speak is a bit odd," Alec replied before Jaime could say anything. "We dinna hold it against her."

"Wonderful," Hilda said, her eyes growing wide. "I have so much to ask you. I have always wanted to go beyond Scotland. Where have ye been? Where are ye from? Where are ye going next?"

"You have many questions!" Jaime laughed. "I will answer them all, I promise, one at a time."

"Thank ye very much," Hilda said, scrunching her nose up.

"Hilda, let's get inside and get Miss Jaime comfortable," Alec said, looking down at his sister as she tugged on his cloak.

"Miss Gillie is inside," she whispered. "And her smelly father."

"Is that so? Well, this should be interesting then," Alec said, forcing a nervous smile. Now that his sisters had seen them, it was too late to turn around, but it would certainly mean speeding up his plan. He hoped Jaime could follow his lead. As they approached the front door, Alec turned quickly to her.

"I need ye to do me a favor. No matter what is said in there, please follow me lead and let me explain later," he said in a low voice, for her ears alone. "Can you promise me that? Then I'll do anything you need."

Jaime only had time to blink in bewilderment before Alec's father approached. She looked at Alec with a quick nod of her head, and he warmed at her trust in him as she straightened and smiled at the man in the doorway. Jaime lacked that wariness when meeting new people, a wariness that Alec had learned was necessary through his years.

Alec turned and threw his shoulders back as he greeted his father.

"Father," Alec said, leaning forward and shaking his hand.

"Where's Balloch and the furs?" his father asked gruffly.

"He'll be along soon. He went on his own to Perth after I was waylaid. Father, this is Jaime of the Abernathy clan," Alec said stepping to the side to allow the two to share greetings. "Jaime this is my father, Laird Cinead McDermont."

"It's nice to meet you," Jaime said, her voice friendly, but Alec could see the apprehension in her eyes at meeting his father. He didn't blame her. Cinead was an intimidating man, one who hid his emotions and made others guess at what he was thinking.

"Aye, well, come inside," Cinead said stepping out of the entrance and eyeing Jaime critically as she passed. "The weather is blustery today."

Alec led the group through the hall and into the parlor, where Alexandra and her father, Rory Gillie, were standing by the fire. Jaime stayed a step behind him, and he knew she must be hidden from view, although he could feel her nervousness at the entire situation. Cinead moved around Alec and stood next to the Gillie laird, glaring at Alec in a threat not to fight the proceedings.

"The Gillies have come to speak of arrangements for the marriage," Cinead stated, his voice suggesting he was not prepared to argue it. "It seems we have come to a worthy agreement of clans."

"It has been a long road," added Rory, "and I hope that ye, lad, will be good to me daughter."

"These arrangements willna be necessary," Alec said, forcing his voice to be steady, even, as unrelenting as his father's. "Though I am sure the Gillie clan would make a fine addition to the McDermonts, I have already chosen a wife. Jaime and I married. I am sorry I had no time to send word."

Cinead's teeth clenched, and his hands balled into fists. Rory's mouth dropped open and he looked at his daughter, Alexandra, who squinted angrily at Jaime, clearly trying to convey her displeasure in Alec's choice. The Gillie laird finally turned back, red-faced, to the couple. Alec stood his ground, his chest taut and his hand around Jaime's wrist. He could feel the rapid beating of her pulse below his fingers, and he attempted to soothe her by pulling her close. He had no allies in this room, and he could only hope the Gillies would leave quietly.

He was to be disappointed.

"This is a great dishonor!" Rory shouted. "Cinead, are ye going let this stand? Surely ye know the consequences of breaking such an arrangement. Who *is* this woman?"

"Are ye threatening my father?" Alec said in a steady voice, one that was, however, laced with anger. "Our clans would never have been at peace, marriage or not. You ken that, I ken that, and I am sure my stepmother did too. All this marriage would do is bring that same conflict into our home. I'd ask ye to leave this house before I take action I regret."

Cinead stood silently, staring at the two of them. He opened his mouth a few times, but no words came out, until he finally ran a hand over his head, accepting that he couldn't fight what his son had done.

Rory took his daughter by the arm and dragged her to the front door, the smug smile now erased from his face. Alexandra, while clearly annoyed that Alec had been the one to turn her down, didn't seem otherwise overly affected. The Laird of the Gillies turned back toward Alec, who had stepped into the hall.

"This will *not* go without retribution," Rory hissed through gritted teeth in a warning before turning and pulling the heavy door shut behind them.

Alec stepped back into the parlor room and stretched his shoulders. He looked up at his father, who he knew would have some choice words for him. Cinead began to walk across the room and stopped, looking Alec in the eyes.

"Do mhàthair a bhiodh fo bhròn. Tha thu air na disgraced dhuinn," his father said forcefully to him in Gaelic before staring at Jaime without any hint of welcome, and then turning and walking out the door, his step rigid and heavy.

"What did he say?" Jaime whispered to Alec, who tried not to let his father's words seep into him and affect his soul.

"Yer mother would be saddened. Ye disgrace us," he replied in a low voice, just above a whisper, no expression on his face as he stared ahead of him.

"Alec," Jaime said, as he saw the pity in her eyes replaced by a slow burn of anger, "Your father's choice of words was unfortunate and likely spoken in anger. But what did you think would come of this? I appreciate you helping me out here, but to tell your *family* we are *married*? It's one thing to lie to the innkeeper or the dressmaker, but Alec, you never said a word to me of this little plan of yours. When did you decide on this scheme? We had fun, yes, but I have a life! One that I cannot just leave to be your bride, especially when you never even asked me to do so."

Alec watched as Jaime pushed past him, dropping her shawl on the floor and stalking out the door into the cold afternoon air. He picked up the garment and chased after her, surprised at the fear of her flight flowing through his chest. He closed the door behind him and looked out at Jaime standing in the yard staring at the sheep grazing in the field, her arms wrapped tightly around herself, for warmth or comfort, he was not sure. He slowly walked up to her and wrapped the shawl around her shivering shoulders. She turned toward him, her expression unrelenting.

"How dare you put me in that position?" she hissed, the outdoors obviously not clearing away her displeasure. "What am I to do now? Leave your family to clean up this mess, or stay and forget everything I am? I don't belong here, Alec, why don't you understand that?"

"You do not even know where home is," he snapped back. "I have just handed ye a life, a good one. Why are ye so angry at me for that?"

Even as he said the words, he hadn't realized until this moment that part of him had held onto the hope that she might, perhaps, never return to whatever life she had left, that she could be happy here, with him. He had never responded to another woman the way he had her, and the idea of her actually being his bride... well, it didn't scare him like it should.

"I am not from here," she cried out. "This is not right, this is not where, or *when*, I am supposed to be. I have a life and friends and... and a life," she finished, though rather miserably.

"You said that," Alec responded. "Please, Jaime, I beg of ye, do this for me for a time. If yer truly from another place, or another time as ye say, then we will all disappear from you when you return. But for me, it will save my family. The Gillies are planning something treacherous, and I need the time to prove it, to ensure our families are *never* merged."

"For how long?" she asked angrily. "Until I am old and gray and don't even recognize home when I go back? All of this is insane."

Alec sighed as Jaime stepped forward, putting her face in

her hands. The idea had seemed so simple before he knew anything about her. Now, however, a burning tinge of guilt and sadness flooded him, and he knew he would eventually have to appease her and go look for this "portal" sorcery she kept speaking of. Knowing that it would at least calm her nerves, Alec stepped forward and placed his hand on her shoulder, seeing the tears in her eyes.

"Please dinna cry," he said gently. "If ye do this for me, for a fortnight, two at most, I promise I shall help ye find yer way back to yer... time."

"You don't even believe me," Jaime scoffed, drying her eyes on her shawl.

"It will nae matter what I believe as long as I do as you wish," he stated. "Help me, and I shall help you."

"Really?" Jaime asked, looking up cautiously from the wrap around her shoulders. "Do you really promise or is this another trick you have cooked up?"

"I promise," he said, standing up straight and sticking his hand out toward her. "I never lie."

"Fine," she said angrily, pushing his hand away. "But so you know, for the future, sleeping with a woman, playing with her heart, that's not the way to get what you want."

Alec's face dropped as soon as her words hit him with their full force. Making love in the woods the night before had never been part of this plan or on his mind. It had happened upon feeling, without thought, and in the light of day he knew he should regret it, but he found that he couldn't wish it away. Guilt that she would feel otherwise surged through his chest as he looked at the small, beautiful woman in front of him, her green eyes darkened in anger, anger that he had caused.

"That was never my intention," he said sadly, shaking his head.

"It… it doesn't matter," she muttered. "Not anymore. It's cold. Will you show me to our room, at least?"

Alec nodded and allowed Jaime to walk ahead toward the house. Her strawberry blonde hair glistened in the sunlight, and at that moment, he started to question the entirety of his plan, which at one time had seemed so sure.

One thing was certain. Wherever this woman had come from, Alec feared she would change his life forever, before returning from whence she came.

CHAPTER 7

Jaime stood in the doorway of the small bedroom that she would now be calling home, at least for a little while. She oddly felt both completely out of place and also at ease in the castle. Perhaps it was because even though she knew she wasn't welcomed, at least not by Alec's father, she had always been drawn to the castles of Scotland, as cold and drafty as they were.

She scanned the space, realizing this was nothing more than a place to sleep for Alec. Back home, her bedroom had always been her sanctuary, and she knew if she kept having to dodge Alec's father and a warring clan, she would need somewhere comfortable to retreat. She pushed the sleeves up on her gown and straightened the covers on the bed. The furniture was beautiful, handcrafted with obvious care. The mattress was situated on a poster bed with hand-carved crests of the McDermont clan etched into the sides. The desk by the window had been built in a similar style, and Jaime appreciated the quality of craftsmanship that was so rare in her own time.

Hilda walked into the room with dresses and blankets

piled so high in her arms that she couldn't see over them all. Her sister, a girl of about fifteen, followed behind her. The older girl was tall and slender with curly red hair that fell to her mid-back. The freckles across her nose and cheeks were the only feature holding her back from looking like a grown woman. Her gentle, welcoming eyes soothed Jaime's nerves, and she took the garments from Hilda with a smile and a thank you before turning to the girl.

"I'm Jaime," she said, infusing as much cheer as she could muster into her voice. "You must be Alec's other sister."

"My name is Una," the girl said sweetly. "It's very nice to meet ye. We brought some dresses for ye, and some extra blankets in case ye get cold."

"That is so kind of you," Jaime replied, setting the clothes down on the bed. "Perhaps you could show me around later today. We could get to know one another."

"Of course," Hilda said sincerely. "Una knows all there is to know about our land and likes to help in the kitchen, even though the cook tries to chase her out. And I can show ye the hiding places I've found, just in case ye ever need them."

"That sounds simply delightful," Jaime responded, laughing at Hilda's impishness. "I'll tell you a secret. I've never been one to enjoy cooking myself."

"Father says I should keep out of the kitchens," Una replied quietly. "Mother loved working in the kitchens, however, and I ken all of the dishes she made. Now that yer part of the family, you can learn them too."

Jaime forced her smile as she stood up straight, uncomfortable with the secret she was hiding, her annoyance with Alec over the lie growing again.

"I must thank you," she said, leaning down to look the girls in the eye. "Your welcome to me is much appreciated."

Hilda nodded, her face a mask of seriousness. "If Alec likes ye, then we do too," she said loyally, before glancing quickly at her sister and then leaning into Jaime, her voice now a whisper. "And anyone would be better than Alexandra Gillie."

"Hilda!" Una gasped as Alec walked through the doorway and clapped his hands together, his own positivity as forced as Jaime's.

Una, however, looked back at him and smiled, her love for her brother obvious. Jaime wondered at the difference in their ages, as she placed Alec about ten years older than his next sister.

"Good morning, my little lasses," Alec said smiling. "Ye shall both have plenty of time to torture Jaime later. I must be getting ready to tend the sheep. Father has left to see to a few things, and he will nae return 'til tomorrow."

"What is Jaime going to do?" Hilda asked with her hands on her hips. "Ye cannae just bring her home and leave her alone in this room. She will be *very* bored."

"I can help with the sheep," Jaime stated.

"I dinna ken if that's something you want to jump right into," Alec responded, Jaime's back stiffening at the censure in his tone. She was not a child and would not be spoken to as such. "Ye dinna seem like a woman who has spent much of her time with animals."

"I'll have you know that I once helped birth not one, but *two* baby calves," Jaime stated with pride, although she did remember a slight bit of queasiness accompanied the entire experience. She had been staying overnight at her friend's farm, and they had been called down to the barn to watch. "I'm pretty sure I can handle some Scottish farm work."

"If yer sure, lass," Alec said with a shrug that made it obvious he had no belief in her whatsoever. "Throw on one of the work dresses me sisters brought you and yer boots, and meet me near the barn when yer ready."

The girls followed Alec out, giggling at one another, while

Jaime changed clothes. The new dress was much more comfortable, lightweight, and easy to move in. It was a dark shade of blue that flowed over her hips down to just below the top of her boots. She found her borrowed cloak and tied it around her neck, making sure she would stay warm. She marched out the front doors of the castle with determination, taking a moment to gather her bearings and determine just which building was the barn. A few moos and a glimpse of Alec's stunning frame finally guided her way.

Jaime took her time meandering into the building, appreciating the view of Alec bent over a pile of material before he straightened and saw her. Jaime enjoyed the fact that, despite their words with one another, seeing her brought a smile to his face.

"We are gonna move the sheep from that enclosure to this one so I can work on the fence," he explained, pointing just outside the door at their outdoor run. "So, basically we chase the sheep into that gate and out into the other enclosure."

"Seems easy enough," Jaime stated, taking a long stick from Alec and looking at it curiously. "I'm not hitting them, am I?"

"No, no. Just tap them a bit, and they will start running," he replied, motioning with his arm. "The trick is to get them all running in the right direction at the same time."

Jaime nodded her head, feeling a bit less confident than she had originally. She walked behind Alec into the large field where the sheep were grazing and watched as he stood behind them and started whistling. As angry as she was at his deception, she couldn't help but admit to herself that he was certainly a fine specimen of a man. The skin of his bared forearms and calves glistened and gave her glimpses of his rippling muscles underneath, her fingers twitching as she remembered her hands on him. As big as he was, he moved deftly and with agility. His movements brought back memories of their night in the woods. Her actions seemed so foolish now. She must have seemed like quite the wanton to have moved on him so quickly, but the magic of the forest and the finest man she had ever met – or conjured up, she still hadn't ruled out the trickery of her own mind – had taken over her that night.

The sheep began to move slowly but not in the direction Alec intended. He looked up at Jaime and motioned to the sheep. She snapped herself back to attention, took a deep breath, and jumped in, tapping the back of the sheep every time they moved the wrong way. Before long, she was running all over the field, whistling at rogue animals and trying to woo them into their new home. She looked up to see Alec standing next to the gate motioning two younger sheep on the side to take the path into the pen.

Jaime took off running after them, moving them in a zigzag pattern through the field. The ground was soft, and her ankles buckled every time she stepped into their tracks. She had grown comfortable walking in the soft leather of the boots, but running in them was something else entirely. She was about to shout in triumph when she saw that they were all heading straight for the opening, but she had planned her celebration too soon, for her foot caught in mud and she slipped, landing hard on her behind.

Jaime said a quick prayer that Alec hadn't seen the debacle, but when she looked up, she saw that he was leaning against the gate, which was closed behind the sheep, grinning at her.

Jaime shot him a wry glance from her seat in a pile of dirt, telling him just what she thought of his reaction.

He walked toward her slowly, the corners of his mouth twitching as he was clearly holding back his laughter, and Jaime appreciated the attempt, even if it was rather pitiful. He reached his hand down to help her up, but even with his strength, she slipped and slid as her boots lost traction, and eventually Alec couldn't hold her any longer, and he fell right on top of her. The two sat in the mud for a moment, stunned, until Alec caught her gaze. His lips quirked for a minute, and then Jaime found she couldn't help it any longer, and at the same time, easy laughter sprang forth from them both.

"Okay, maybe not as easy as I thought," Jaime said through her laughter. "But I did it."

"Ye did," Alec stated, bracing himself to stand. "I had faith the whole time."

"Liar," Jaime whispered, smiling as Alec pulled her to her feet. "Oh no."

Alec looked at Jaime's disappointed face and followed her eyes over to the left side of the field. There was a small lamb standing in the mud, looking around in wonderment – perhaps at his freedom, perhaps at his confusion as to where the rest of his family had gone. Alec smiled at Jaime's scrunched up nose and disappointment.

"It's the baby," Alec replied. "He was born right before I left. He'll be fine while I fix the fence."

"Can I pet him?" Jaime asked, feeling a sense of kinship with the animal.

"Of course," Alec responded with a shrug. "They really are gentle creatures — not at all like you."

"Right," Jaime responded, rolling her eyes as she elbowed Alec in the side. "Go on and fix your fence. I have a little lamb to play with."

"Aye, lass," Alec responded, playfully bowing and heading off across the field.

Jaime watched Alec trot across the yard, his strong muscles rippling through his white blouse, the shape of his thigh muscles apparent through what she now knew was called a "great plaid." She had always appreciated the well-known kilts on the Highlanders of the movies, but she never would have guessed she'd find a man in a blanket so sexy. She scoffed at her lust, pushing it to the side as she carefully approached the puffball of a sheep standing in the field, bleating for company. She ran her hands carefully over the tuft of wool attached to baby's back, and he reached back and licked her hand.

She smiled at him, and all the emotions of the past few weeks came flooding through her. She was so alone here. Just like this lamb in the middle of the enclosure. Even what she thought she'd had with Alec had been nothing more than him using her to buy himself some time as he searched for answers and kept himself unmarried. The worst of it, though? It was no better at home. The melancholy began at her heart and slowly began to pulse through her body, as she took solace in petting the young lamb as if it were a kitten.

As the minutes ticked by and the wide eyes of the baby sheep punctured Jaime's heart, tears began to stream down her face. She missed everything that was familiar back home in her own time. When she had been home, she couldn't wait to get away from it all. She had come farther than she ever dreamed possible, and now she missed it all too much. All she wanted was to be sitting in front of a fireplace, started with matches or a lighter, drinking a cup of hot tea that had been made with an electric kettle, with her parents beside her.

Jaime looked up at the horizon, confused on how she could find this place so warm and inviting but at the same time yearn for her life back. As Alec approached, the lamb left her, letting out a bleat as it ran toward the gate to join its family.

"What has happened? Are you hurt?" Alec said, rushing forward when he noted her tears, lifting her from the ground when he saw her face.

"Bob," she mumbled through tears. "He reminded me of home."

"Who is Bob?" Alec stated, looking around for a man.

"Bob is the baby sheep," she said, pulling back and wiping the tears from her eyes.

"Ye named the sheep?" Alec asked, scrunching his nose. "It is not good to name your food."

"You will not eat Bob!" Jaime shouted, standing back. "Oh, Alec, promise me you won't eat him."

"'Tis what happens to most animals here, love," Alec said, trying to control a smile. "But if it means that much to ye, I'll mark Bob as a wool sheep. Though she might prefer a more feminine name."

Jaime began to laugh through her tears and wrapped her arms around Alec, laying her cheek against his warm chest. They stood for a moment in the cold wind, sharing a connection that eased her homesickness and reminded her that home was where someone made it. Jaime felt Alec pull back and she looked up into his big hazel eyes.

"Why dinna we get ourselves cleaned up, pack some food, and go out to the cliffs to watch the sunset?" Alec offered.

"Okay," Jaime sniffled. "Please tell me there is clean water to get this mud off of me."

"Not here. We never bathe," he said with his arm around her shoulders as they walked toward the house.

"What?" she said staring up at him in surprise, then blushing at her gullibility when he began to laugh.

Once they were back at the house, Alec was all gentleman, bending and helping Jaime take off her muddy boots, setting them outside of the door. She watched as he untied his own and placed them beside hers before opening the door and allowing her to walk in first. The girls rushed to the door and immediately began helping Jaime, seemingly fascinated by her.

"What happened to you?" Hilda gaped, even as Una elbowed her in the side.

"I had a run in with the mud," Jaime said with a sigh.

"Girls, perhaps you could help Jaime get cleaned up?" Alec suggested, and they nodded happily as they led Jaime up the stairs toward her bedroom.

Jaime sat as Una dipped her hair into a bowl of water and worked the mud from the roots. She was a gentle girl, and Jaime imagined she must have been a lot like their mother. Una smiled down at Jaime as she combed the tangles and knots from her strawberry hair and dried it with a woolen cloth. Jaime sat up and ran her fingers through it, surprised at how soft it was and how good it smelled.

"How did you get it so soft? I am assuming you don't have shampoo," Jaime asked, looking in the mirror.

"What is sham...poo?" Una asked.

"Oh, nothing," Jaime replied, realizing she slipped up. "Just a fancy soap."

"Well, my mother had lavender oil she used to wear in her hair, and I figured you might like some," Una explained. "Alec loves lavender. And given that he loves you, I think he would like ye to wear it."

"I'm not sure I would say that he *loves* me," Jaime hedged. "Why do you say that?"

"Well," Una said wiping her hands and walking over to the window. "He married you for one. He did not want to be married, although Father told him he didn't have a choice in the matter when it came to the alliance with the Gillies. But 'tis more than that. I see it when he looks at you. Ye do not notice, but I certainly have never seen him look at Miss Gillie or any of the other woman in that way."

Jaime sat quietly, unsure of what to say as she finished drying her hair. She had only just met the man. Una must have a romantic spirit to imagine such fanciful thoughts.

Jaime stood up and walked over to the dresses on the bed, picking out one that was a little prettier than the others. She stood looking down at the clothing, lost in her thoughts.

"I suppose I should leave you now," Una said, tearing Jaime away from her daydreams. "Alec will have yer meal ready to take with ye. Perhaps next time we can accompany you. 'Tis beautiful, what he wants to show ye."

"Thank you, sweet Una," Jaime replied, smiling kindly, before changing into the new dress, her heart beating slightly faster as she anticipated the time alone with Alec.

CHAPTER 8

When Jaime stepped outside of the castle, dressed without her boots, she found Alec standing there, staring off at the sun slowly setting over the hills in the distance. Jaime stood for a moment, appreciating the view of his side profile. He had what appeared to be a large plaid in one hand, a basket in the other. She couldn't help but admit what a fine-looking man he was, but it was more than that. He stirred something within her, something that made her wish she could take his hand and return with him to the 21st century.

For she had finally come to the realization that this was no dream. There was too much she had discovered, too much that she had no prior knowledge of, nor could even have found deep in her subconscious. Somehow, she had, inconceivably, traveled back to the 1500s.

And found the man of her dreams.

Alec must have sensed her approach, for he turned his head toward her, and she smiled at the welcoming, appreciative look in his eyes as he regarded her – a look that she had yet to see from him. He set his things down and bent to help her with her boots, which were no longer caked in mud.

He must have cleaned them while she was getting ready, for they looked nearly as they had when he had first given them to her.

He bent before her, gently taking her foot in his hand and fitting it into the boot before tying the lace for her, and somehow his touch on the boot was as tender as if he had been stroking his hand across her skin. When he was done tying the laces, she leaned over and kissed him on the cheek. He looked up at her with his brow furrowed, questions in his eyes, but said nothing as he stood and helped her up, gathering his items in one hand as he held out the other to her. They walked along the path which led toward Perth, quiet but enjoying each other's company.

After a few minutes, Alec led her off the path and carefully through the woods. She didn't know where they were going, but she still trusted him, a feeling that surprised her given his recent deception. At least she knew that he wouldn't get them so lost that they would end up in another century entirely.

She looked ahead at a hole in the forest, the lessening light leading the way. Jaime smiled at Alec as he stood to the side and helped her up and over a fallen tree into the light. She gasped as she stared out over the cliffs. The sun was inching toward the horizon, casting reflections of oranges, pinks, and browns down across the rippling water. The breeze picked up, and the smell of salt and sea filled Jaime's nose.

This, apparently, was where they were stopping for the meal as Alec flung the blanket out in front of *him*, laying it upon the ground before he went to work unpacking the basket of fruits, cheeses, oatcakes, and some cured sausages. He pulled out a flask of wine and set it down next to the food before reaching for Jaime's hand and helping her down onto the blanket. Jaime ran her hands over the soft fur beneath her as she looked out over the incredible blue-green of the water. It was absolutely beautiful. There were no boats or telephone wires; there were no lights from the city or passing cars; just all natural beauty. She closed her eyes and felt the salty air hit her skin, smiling at the comfort she felt deep in her chest, a comfort that had been missing for so long she hadn't even realized it had left.

Jaime and Alec sat, eating the food, laughing at the day's events and watching the sun lower into the Scottish horizon. Jaime scooted nearer to Alec, feeling close to him on the high cliffs. He put his arm around her and kissed her on the top of the head, as they both seemed to want to linger, avoiding the end of the evening. Jaime sighed, lost in her thoughts, before turning to Alec.

"I've been thinking," she began, and Alec tilted his head to the side as he regarded her, waiting for her to continue.

"Your family and the Gillies think we are married. We've come this far. I'd like to know that your family name is protected even after I have left," she said, then hurried to continue before he could say anything. "If— if you'll have me, if you'd like it, I will marry you, here and now, in this time. Let there be a record of it, so that no one can deny it. Then after I leave—well, you can make up a story, have me declared dead after a time, I suppose."

"Me father already spoke to me about this," Alec said looking out over the water. "He may not be pleased with our union, but as it is already so, he would like us to have a real ceremony so that the family can be witnesses. I had planned to ask ye tonight if ye would agree. That is why my father is in Perth. He is gathering goods for the feast. He wants to hold it on the morrow before sunset."

"Oh," Jaime said, sitting up, away from him, her spine

straightening. She had thought on this for so long, yet wasn't prepared for such immediacy. "Tomorrow? Well, then, I suppose my thoughts didn't much matter. Um, good. Okay. Tomorrow it is."

Alec smiled distractedly and Jaime turned back toward the ocean, confusion settling in her soul. She had just met Alec, but here, after just a few days in 16th century Scotland, she felt she knew him better than she had known Chris after *years* of dating. Perhaps it was the fact they had been forced together in close proximity, with no cell phones or other media to distract them from one another. Perhaps it was because they were pretending to be married. She wasn't sure, but her heart fluttered, knowing she was setting herself up for heartbreak, still unsure if the man she had grown close to, the man she would marry, believed her at all.

She had imagined her wedding day so many times, but never had it included marriage to a sexy Highlander she had just met in 1544.

When the sun finally set over the water in front of them, they packed up their things and walked quietly back to the house. There was a tenseness between them upon this return journey, with so many emotions and words hovering in the air between them but left unsaid for fear of what they might mean.

Jaime, lost in her thoughts, clasped the blanket to her chest as they walked. Alec seemed distracted, almost like he wasn't there at all. Jaime's chest ached as she was so torn between wanting to give herself to this man yet wanting to run for Crieff and find the portal, as she had taken to calling wherever she had slipped through time, so she could soon be happily tucked back into her bed at her cottage, back to the comfort of the place and time she had always known.

But she didn't know if that was even an option – or if she could be happy without Alec by her side.

Once in the castle, Jaime changed into the nightgown she had been given and pulled herself under the covers, Alec's warm body next to her – so close, and yet so far away. He was lying on his back, his arms behind his head, still seemingly lost in his own thoughts. Jaime turned away from him and lay on her side, hoping sleep would take her, rescuing her from her jumbled thoughts and anxieties. The bed rustled as Alec turned toward her, his warm skin rubbing against her legs, just touching her, although he made no attempt to come any closer. She lay still until she heard his deepened breathing and then turned over and placed her head on his chest. His heart beat methodically beneath her ear, and to the sound of her future husband's chest, she fell deep into sleep, dreams of her home and her friends interspersed with dreams of Alec, the Highland warrior, filling the space between asleep and awake.

She tossed and turned throughout the night until the light started to seep in through the windows. Jaime lifted her head from Alec's chest and looked out at the bright, cold day. Her eyes fell upon Alec's sleeping face, and for a moment, she felt content, like she had finally found where she belonged. Which was ridiculous. She didn't belong here. She belonged in the time in which she was born. She sighed and sat up on the edge of the bed, looking out the window on the fields that stretched before her as she contemplated the day that lay ahead.

Today she would become a wife. Today, incredibly, was her wedding day.

CHAPTER 9

"Wake up, sleepyhead," a small voice whispered into Jaime's ear, not realizing that Jaime had already been wide awake for a time. "It's yer wedding day. Well, again."

Jaime turned to see Hilda and Una staring at her excitedly. She couldn't help but smile softly in return, their impatience and enthusiasm almost contagious. Una stood holding yet another blue dress in her arms while Hilda held a wreath of flowers and pair of satin slippers. They walked quickly over to the table and set them down as Jaime pulled herself from the bed, noticing Alec was gone. The sun was shining, although there were a few dark clouds in the distance. Nerves began to tingle in Jaime's belly.

"Jaime," Hilda said, the girl's bossy tone making Jaime smile. "This is how it works, if you dinna ken. Ye can go break your fast, and then 'tis hair and dressing time, followed by a ride to the church."

Both girls appeared to already have dressed for the occasion in dresses far more elaborate than Jaime had yet seen them wear.

"Sounds good," Jaime said apprehensively. "Are there going to be a lot of people?"

"Of course," Una laughed. "It's a McDermont celebration. Everyone who could make it this quickly will be here! Is yer family coming?"

"No," Jaime responded swiftly. "They are… too far away." She put on the robe the girls had brought to her and followed them into the dining area.

The house appeared to be empty besides the three of them, the cook, and the few servants of the household. Jaime figured the men were setting up for the day. She heard a loud banging from outside and walked to the door, opening it slightly to peek out. Alec was standing on a large block, hammering an overhang together. There were handmade tables all around with beautiful linens covering each, a cleared area in the center that Jaime assumed was for dancing. Apparently 16th century Highland weddings were not much different from the ones in her time.

When Jaime was done eating, she went back into the bedroom, where Una was standing with what looked like a hot curling iron contraption, and Hilda was laying out different jars on the counter. The thought of a child putting a hot curling iron from the fire in her hair terrified Jaime, and she laughed in nervousness.

"I thought since my hair is already wavy that maybe we don't curl it," Jaime suggested. "I like the natural look."

Una looked at her with some confusion, but shrugged her shoulders and set the iron down on the bricks of the fireplace to cool. Relieved she wasn't going to have to endure the hot iron, Jaime sat down in the chair and let the girls apply whatever was in the jars in front of them to her face. They lightly dabbed and polished for what seemed like forever, standing back like artists examining their work after each swish of their brush. It reminded Jaime of the time she had let her cousin's daughter apply her make-up, only this time, it seemed the girls knew what they were doing. Finally, after hours of primping and pinning of hair, Hilda announced it was time to put the dress on.

"First you have to finish this last stitch of the dress for good luck," Una explained. "This was Alec's mother's wedding dress. I've fixed it a bit to fit you."

"Oh Una, that is so incredibly sweet of you, but it is not at all necessary. I-I don't know if I should. I can wear something else," said Jaime as she looked at the intricate overlay of lace, convinced that it would fall apart at her touch, but when she saw Una's face fall, she realized she had said the wrong thing. "But, of course, if you think I should, then I'll wear it. It's absolutely stunning Una, really. You are very talented."

"Thank you," Una said, now beaming. "It is perfect for a woman joining the McDermont clan."

Jaime smiled at Una's wisdom. The girl spoke as if she had rehearsed that very speech in her chambers. Hilda stood smiling approvingly and nodding feverishly, obviously excited to see what Jaime would look like in the gown. Jaime took the needle from Una and finished the stitch as instructed. She breathed a sigh of relief when Una nodded approvingly. Jaime knew how to fix a hole in her pants, but she was certainly no seamstress. Jamie passed the needle back and peered up at the girls.

"Well, let's give it a try then, shall we?" Jaime said, watching the girls nod excitedly.

She snuck behind the dressing partition and noticed they had placed a long mirror inside for her to see herself in. It was the first time she remembered really looking at herself in a long while. She slipped her nightgown off and pulled the dress over her head, reaching to lace the sides. The gown had a high square top that stopped right at the collarbone and led straight into the long delicate sleeves. It was form fitting and hugged her curves down to the waist where it flared out ever so slightly. The material on the bottom was silk, but it had a lace overlay that ran from top to bottom.

Jaime turned and froze, staring at herself in the mirror. The girls had pinned half of her hair back in a halo-like style, the waves trickling down over her shoulders. Her cheeks were rosy from the makeup they had applied, and her lips were a subtle pink. The dress fit her perfectly, as if Una had made it for her. A tear popped in the corner of her eye as she thought about her mother and father seeing her in this dress. Even across timelines, she would never be able to bring them back.

As she stepped out from behind the partition, the girls clapped excitedly, and Jaime could see the look of pride on Una's face. Una walked over and lifted the long train and flipped it over, revealing a stitched horseshoe on the bottom. She smiled and handed the edge of the fabric to Jaime to inspect.

"I thought it might be cumbersome to carry a horseshoe for luck, so I etched one in the dress instead," she explained.

"Thank you so much, both of you," said Jaime, as she slipped the shoes Hilda had held out toward her onto her feet. "You have really thought of everything, haven't you?"

"Almost," Una said smiling as she reached for the bedroom door. "Alec has a gift for ye."

Jaime watched as Una covered her brother's eyes and backed him into the room, so he would not see his bride before the church. He chuckled as the girls scurried around him. When his steps faltered and he sniffed the air, Jaime did the same, catching the subtle hints of lavender and rose the girls had used on her.

"This was my mother's," Alec said as he held out a necklace for Jaime to take. "I thought ye might wear it for the ceremony."

"Oh, it's beautiful," Jaime gasped as she took the long silver chain from Alec's outstretched arm. The green stone of the pendant sparkled in the light. "Thank you."

"I shall see ye at the chapel?" he asked, the slight quiver in his voice revealing his uncertainty.

"You shall," she replied, leaning in and kissing him on the cheek.

Una showed him to the door, and Jaime couldn't help herself from drifting to the window, watching as he effortlessly jumped on a horse beside his brother and father and began to trot down the path toward what she assumed was the chapel in Perth.

Una squealed in excitement. "Father has readied the horse-drawn carriage," she blurted in the doorway to the chambers. "Hilda, carry the flowers for Jaime, it's time to depart."

Jaime watched, nearly feeling like a spectator through all of the preparations as Hilda ran off to the kitchen, returning with a bouquet of small white flowers wrapped in ribbon. Jaime smiled as she took them and held them tightly in one hand while rolling the emerald stone of her necklace around in her other. Jaime stepped out into the hallway and walked toward the door, her nerves so on edge she feared she might throw up. Hilda carried the train of her gown out the door to avoid getting it dirty, and the three girls climbed into the carriage. Jaime looked around at the satin-lined walls and cushioned seats and felt like the Queen riding to her castle. The McDermont Clan shield hung proudly over the small door and just below the window of the carriage was a beautifully carved Celtic knot.

"This carriage is our clan's," Una explained. "Anyone who gets married or dies gets to use it. At funerals, they pull the casket on a wagon behind the carriage, and everything is draped in clan colors."

"Wow," Jaime said, realizing sadly that Una likely only knew this because of her mother's death.

Jaime stared out the carriage window as they rode, listening to the clopping of the horse's hooves along the dirt road to Perth. The scenery flew by quickly as they picked up the pace and Jaime could smell a hint of salt from the sea in the air as they passed the spot where Alec had taken her into the forest and to the cliffs. As they rode through the town center of Perth, onlookers pointed and waved as the carriage passed by. Jaime looked up ahead, her stomach flip-flopping at the stone chapel rising up before them, large in comparison to its surrounding buildings. Guests were entering through the doorways.

"When we arrive, you are to walk on the right side of the church down and around three times," Una instructed. "It is customary. Alec told me you had never been to a wedding, so he asked that I give ye all the information."

"That was kind of him," Jaime said, trying not to let the girl hear any annoyance in her voice, for she did truly appreciate Una's thoughtfulness. But why had Alec himself not told her any of this? While she realized that obviously much had changed in the way women were treated over the past five hundred and some years. Alec had seemed different somehow. "Will you be with me?"

"Oh, no. We wait by the doors for you," Hilda cut in. "It's yer time with God."

"I see," Jaime said nodding her head.

When the carriage came to a stop, a tall man with a long fiery beard dressed in clan colors opened the door and helped Jaime down. She watched as the girls exited the carriage, each pulling on the man's beard, inciting laughter. He looked at Jaime and smiled, offering his arm for her to take.

"Me name is Ainsley, of the McDermont clan," the man

explained with a jolly tone. "Alec explained yer father had passed and ye would need someone to hand ye over, so I am here to do the duty, if ye will have me."

"I would be honored," Jaime stated, choking back tears. She didn't understand why she was so emotional about all of this, as it was all for show and it would soon be nothing but a memory that lived centuries in the past.

"Well, I'll be waiting here for when yer done," he said looking ahead at the church, and then suddenly, Jaime was alone once more.

CHAPTER 10

✑

*J*aime didn't know if she had ever been so nervous as she was in this moment. She began to walk down the right side of the building, shivering slightly from the cold wind. By the third lap, Jaime was ready to get inside, the cold air biting at her through the thin lace. As she made her final walk toward Ainsley, she closed her eyes and told herself to just enjoy this.

She walked back up to the round jolly man and smiled. He kissed her on the cheek and gave her a quick nod. Jaime nervously took his arm, and he patted her hand kindly, as though sensing her fears. Bagpipes and flutes began to play as she stepped over the threshold of the church and laughter could be heard as the girls made their way down the aisle.

Then it was Jaime's turn. She stepped onto the large round stones that made up the floor and walked carefully, afraid to look up at Alec. About halfway down, she finally glanced to the front, and the scene before her washed the nerves away. Alec was standing tall at the front, dressed in a white blouse and draperies signifying his clan and his role within it. His long, red-tinged hair framed his chiseled face, and his gaze never wavered as he stared at her walking toward him.

Butterflies of a different sort began flapping their wings excitedly within Jaime's stomach.

When they reached the front, Ainsley handed her to Alec, and as he retreated, Jaime stepped forward and faced the man about to become her husband, clasping his hands tightly. Much of the ceremony was in Gaelic, but they switched to English when it was time for her to give her oath. It was short and sweet, and when done, Hilda walked forward, handing them each a silver ring. Jaime looked up into Alec's eyes as they each placed a ring on one another's finger. When it was done, Alec's father approached and performed the hand tying ceremony, his face void of emotion. At its completion, the priest gave his blessing, and Alec looked at Jaime, seemingly taken aback by the tears that flowed down her cheeks, a look of concern crossing his face. He pressed his lips against hers, pulling her close.

When the ceremony was complete, the girls joined Alec and Jaime in the carriage as they returned to the house for what Jaime would call a reception. The carriage ride was quiet except for Hilda chattering on about the number of guests and how beautiful Jaime was and wasn't it the loveliest of services and so on. Over her prattling, Alec reached over and took Jaime's hand, squeezing it tightly before leaning in.

"Thank you," he whispered in her ear.

Jaime nodded, unable to summon a smile to her face as her stomach had tightened into a bundle of nerves as the weight of today descended upon her, as well as the thought of what was to come next.

She realized then that she had been hoping Alec would say something to her that was less about his clan and much more about romance, which was ridiculous. She had suggested this as much as he, and she would be going home any time now. She just wondered, deep within her, if he actually cared about her or just saw her as a piece of his plan.

When they arrived home, they waited in the carriage until everyone else slowly meandered in and seated themselves at the long tables. Jaime lined up with her new husband and walked behind his father in the traditional Scottish march. They were to immediately begin their first dance and Jaime tried her best to follow along.

"Alec," she murmured as he swept her up into his arms.

"Yes, wife?" his voice grumbled in her ear.

"I have no idea how to dance."

His arms tightened around her in a surge of protectiveness.

"Not to worry, lass – I've got you."

Before saying another word, he scooped her up in his arms, slowly moving around the dance floor. Jaime couldn't have said whether he was keeping the right time to the music, but it didn't matter. Not when he was looking into her eyes so intensely that it sent chills through her entire body, chills that had nothing to do with the rather frigid temperature of the day. The Highlanders were much tougher than Jaime could ever profess to being.

When the dance finished, Alec set her down gently on her feet, stepping toward her as one hand came underneath her chin. When he tilted her head up toward him, Jaime's lips parted, ready, waiting for his kiss. Alec's eyes gleamed as though he was somewhat surprised, but just as he leaned in, a loud cheer resounded behind him, and a hand so large that Jaime expected to see that they had been overrun by giants wrapped over his shoulder.

"A toast!" A large, burly man shouted, and with a smile of apology, Alec was gone, stolen away from her by his own clan members. Jaime, however, didn't mind. For if Alec's clan was happy, then she – they – had succeeded.

It was the last Jaime saw of Alec for a long while, as the celebration stretched on into the night. Jaime spent most of it sitting, quietly watching rapturously as the men and women danced merrily to traditional music. Their feet were flying, their plaids flapping, wide, heady grins on their faces as they spun in time to the music. Jaime couldn't remember a time she had ever seen such joy so openly celebrated.

There were lots of toasts, especially once the lagers had flowed. Ainsley had just stood to say something when Jaime caught the back of Alec's head disappearing into the castle beyond. She drifted toward the entryway, telling herself that she should wait, that he would return and find her soon enough, but she couldn't help that she was so drawn to him that her feet practically carried her toward him of their own accord.

It was just that she... missed him.

She pushed away the niggling doubt in her mind of what she was going to do once she returned to her own time, of whether she would miss him still when it was years between them instead of hours. Telling herself she was being ridiculous, Jaime pushed open the great door at the front of the building, quickly hearing shouting from within. She slid through the door, slinking into the shadows of the great room as Alec's voice turned into a mutter and his father started up instead.

"I canna provide my blessing for I dinna understand why ye did this," Alec's father bellowed. "She looks and talks like a bloody English. How do ye know she's not? She didna have any family here. What kind of woman has no family? I'll tell you – the kind with something to hide."

Jaime's hands balled into fists at her side. There were many things she would allow others to say about her. Comments about her family were not included.

"Actually, sir," Jaime realized belatedly that she probably

shouldn't call an English-hating clan leader, 'sir,' but it was too late now. "I am the kind that has lost her family to tragedy." As they two men searched for the source of her voice in the shadows, Jaime stepped out from the doorway and into the hall. "I am from the Abernathy... clan, and am the last of us left – at least, the last that I know of. Trust me, I would never, ever choose to be alone like this. But now, under God's grace, I have Alec. And Una and Hilda and... and you as well, sir, if you'll have me."

Cinead was practically shaking with his anger, but Jaime refused to back away from where he stood with his huge hands balled up on his hips. For it wasn't just Cinead that caught her attention, but Alec, and the look of proud encouragement that he sent her way – one that meant everything to her. Cinead looked from one of them to the other, at the stare neither of them could seem to break, and threw his hands in the air as he walked out the door. He paused as he looked back at them – first at Jaime, then at Alec, his brow furrowed and the weight of his entire clan on his shoulders.

"Yer foolery has cost us peace," he growled. "And if the death of a McDermont comes by the hand of a Gillie, well, that blood will be on *you* and yer love of a bonnie face."

The moment he stormed away, Alec was moving, across the parlor toward Jaime, taking her hands in his. He tilted her head up to look at him in that way of his, the one that seemed to tell her without words just how much she meant to him, even if neither of them was brave enough to say it in the face of all they stood against. But the truth was, Jaime thought as she blinked back tears, it had all become too much, and as tired as she was, the censure of Alec's father was nearly enough to completely undo her.

Alec pushed a tendril of hair from her face, wrapping it around her ear, before he leaned down and softly took her lips.

"Dinna mind my father. He's more bluff than any action. He's too blinded by his own grief to understand that this will be for the best in the end. But I think the revelries are over for me," Alec said, his voice dropping to a whisper by the end. "What do ye say I take my wife to bed?"

Jaime nodded, unsure if he meant only sleep, but wanting so much more than that. The butterfly wings began to flutter rapidly within her again, as all of the memories of the last time they had made love came rushing back. This time would be different. While they hadn't known one another long, it could no longer be the rushed, frantic meeting of two strangers who were physically attracted to one another. No, this would be the meeting of two souls, husband and wife, who had come to know much more of the other. The truth was, as much as Jaime anticipated making love with him again, it also terrified her, for she couldn't imagine falling for him even harder, knowing how much it would hurt to land when it was all over.

"It will be all right, lass," he said, apparently reading the emotions playing out within her as he took her hand and squeezed it, leading her down the hall to the bedroom, where it appeared fresh linens had been laid out. Alec closed the door quietly and turned to Jaime. "I've got you."

She nodded, trusting him completely, and he turned her around, beginning to slowly unlace the sides of her dress as reverently as if he was unwrapping a priceless gift.

"Let me help you," he said, his voice just above a whisper, as he bent down and lifted the bottom of the gown, pulling it up and over Jaime's head before draping it over the partition. When he turned back, his cheeks reddened as his gaze slid over Jaime's body.

"No undergarments," he said, before his face broke out into a smile. "Yer the best gift a man could ever ask for."

Jaime slipped her shoes off and stood nervously in front

of him, wondering if the standard of the beauty was the same here in 16th century Scotland as it was five hundred years in the future. Whatever Alec saw, however, he seemed happy with, for after a moment of his gaze wandering from her head to her toes, he was moving toward her, placing one hand on her waist, the other on her cheek as he pressed his lips hard against hers. Slowly she moved her hands upward, removing his sashes and breaking from him long enough to lift his shirt over his head. She turned and stepped backward toward the bed as he kicked his boots off, standing strong and naked in front of her, his muscles rippling in the firelight, the finest specimen of a man Jaime had ever seen.

Jaime sat on the edge of the bed and pushed herself backward, spreading her legs to invite him over. He gave a bit of a growl as he prowled toward her, nipping at the inside of her thighs, crawling up her body to rain kisses down her neck, her shoulder, his lips grazing over her breasts so softly, yet causing enough sensation for her to rise up from the bed with a moan. He reached down between them, stroking her at her center. Surely he must feel how ready she was for him. He must have, for she gasped when he pushed inside of her, apparently not having any more patience to wait. She grabbed onto his shoulders as their bodies moved rhythmically in the shadow of the flames.

He reached under her, picking her up, and leaning backward on his knees. She moved her hips against him as she felt the pleasure rising. As her climax came to a crescendo, Jaime leaned back herself, closing her eyes and moaning in pleasure. Alec pushed her down on the bed and continued, thrusting harder and harder as his lips sought hers, mimicking the love play between them. She could feel him swell inside of her as he reached his own peak, groaning in her ear before collapsing to the side of her.

They lay intertwined in each other, her once meticulously

coiffed hair now flowing around them, each of them covered in the glow of the aftermath of sex and satisfaction. Alec stroked her hair as they lay together in silence for a few minutes before he kissed the top of her head.

"Do Scottish men still wear plaids?" he finally asked after a few minutes, and Jaime's lips curled up in a smile at the question, because of what it meant – he believed her or was, at least, willing to humor her.

"In a sense," she said, which only fueled more of his questions. She couldn't say how long they lay there together as he came up with new questions to ask her about her time.

One by one, she would answer, with some funny story or current future event to back up her thoughts. She could see his eyes grow bigger every time she would tell a story about a future political event or war, although she was careful to leave out anything she knew about Scotland, not wanting to scare him or dramatically change the course of time.

"I didna believe you," Alec confessed. "But now, hearing yer stories, I…."

Alec's voice trailed off, and they both sat up at the sound of shouting outside. Jaime's stomach dropped as Alec's father yelled out, the name on his lips echoing through the castle.

The Gillies had arrived, and not to congratulate them.

CHAPTER 11

Alec didn't need to hear anything more than the very first shout to know what was happening – and what he had to do.

He didn't even think as he jumped from the bed, wrapping his plaid around him as he stepped into his boots and drew his sword from the table across the room. He was about to run out the door when he realized that this would be the last place Jaime should stay, for it was the first place the Gillies would look for her.

Fortunately, she had the wherewithal to dress herself, though it was back in her wedding dress, the quickest thing she could find. She nodded at him in understanding, and he was flooded with gratefulness that she wasn't one of those empty-headed women who needed constant direction.

Keeping one arm behind him to ensure she stayed with him, he slowed when he reached the door so that he could look out to make sure the long corridor before them was empty. Satisfied, they hurried around the corner and down the stairs, finding that the shouts and clash of swords were coming from outside.

Still ensuring Jaime was behind him in order to best protect her, Alec walked across the threshold – and found chaos reigning in front of him.

His hands tightened into balls of anger, one at his side, the other fisting his sword. In front of him, Rory Gillie and his clan were facing off with the McDermont men, who were backed by the clans who had been camped out for the night after attending the wedding. At least the women and children seemed to have fled, and he could only hope that none of the Gillies had followed. He only wished that Jaime was with them, far from here.

"Go into the castle and hide," Alec ordered Jaime over his shoulder in a tone that meant no argument. Somehow from amidst the fray, Rory sensed him and stopped, backing away from his foe after he felled him, looking up at Alec with a sneer as he marched toward him.

"Well, well," Rory said gleefully, his eyes manic. "The little laird has decided to come out and play."

"You dinna belong here," Alec bellowed. "This is not yer land. Leave us."

"You need to teach yer son some manners," Rory said, and Alec's heart dropped when he saw his father stepping toward them, his hand on his sword. He had no intention of letting his father fight his battles for him.

"Yer issue is with me, not me father," Alec called out as he moved as quickly as he could toward Rory, cutting off Cinead. The battle raging around them slowed as the men seemed to sense the confrontation about to commence. The Gillies began to step forward, prepared to back their leader, but Rory put his hand up to halt them as Alec stood inches from his face, tensed and ready.

"Ye think he can bring an Englishwoman into our midst, marry her," Rory motioned behind Alec as he closed his eyes for a moment in chagrin, knowing without turning around that Jaime hadn't listened to him, but followed him out, "And change everything we agreed on? Renege on your word?"

"I never had an agreement with ye," Alec said through clenched teeth.

"Ye sound like yer father," Rory hollered back. "Never an agreement. It's history all over again. Did ye ken yer mother was to be mine, boy? But then Cinead McDermont showed some interest in her and she changed her allegiance just as quickly as you have now. It took years, but she *learned*. She learned not to make a fool of Rory Gillie. Yer going to learn the same."

"I know ye killed her, ye bastard," Alec growled, leaning into Rory, the fury raging in his breast ready to be unleashed. He would have sunk his sword straight into the man, but first he needed to hear his confession.

"I wouldna say it was on purpose," Rory replied a sick, wicked grin on his face. "But when we found the wench tripped up and bleeding in the forest – she said it was an accident while she was out foraging, but who is to say for sure? – I cannae say we did much to help."

"So why try to arrange this marriage with Alexandra? How does that help ye?"

"It helps me when yer *dead*, which would have been easy enough to arrange with my daughter as yer wife."

Alec was nearly blinded by the depths of Rory's treachery – so much so that he didn't realize what was happening in front of him until it was too late.

Rory attempted to slyly reach back and pluck a dagger from his belt, but before Alec could react, Cinead must have seen it first, having a better view from his vantage. For as Alec's hand came to the hilt of his sword, Cinead pushed him aside, and launched himself forward, wrestling the Gillie laird to the ground. As they moved and tumbled over each other, fists flying, their swords on the ground at their sides, skirmishes around them began to break out once more. Before Alec could move to help his father, Rory's son had come toward him, and even if he wanted to, Alec was helpless to do anything but keep himself alive.

Alec finally fought him off, his sword slicing through the skin of the man's arm. It wouldn't kill him, but nor would it allow him to fight any longer. Alec took a step back, taking in the scene before him, his shoulders setting in satisfaction as it seemed the McDermonts were handily winning. If only he could find his father. He looked from one side of the hill to the other, searching out Cinead.

It was Rory he saw first. The Gillie laird was rushing forward through the melee, men avoiding him as though sensing his danger and power. What caught Alec was the look of fear upon his face. His head was swiveling, tracking the number of McDermont men and their kin who were swiftly overcoming them, until he hollered out a retreat, running from the grounds with his clan in tow.

"Alec!" His initial smugness fled when Jaime's call cut through the night air, and Alec's heart leapt in his throat as he turned to the sound of her voice, his heart beating rapidly in his chest as he tried to push away the images of the very worst that could have happened to her.

But when he saw her, he realized that she was completely fine – but for the horrified stare that was directed at the ground below them. He followed it, seeing what Jaime was staring at, what his entire clan was now surrounding him to take in.

His father, lying on the ground, blood spread around him.

Cinead reached his arm up for Alec, gasping for air as the dagger sat, pushed into his chest.

Defeated, all emotion seeping out of his body, Alec

dropped to his knees next to his father, knowing that right now, all he could do was be here for Cinead's goodbye, and remember everything as vividly as he could of and for this man. Cinead grabbed Alec's shoulder and brought him closer.

"Father, I'm so sorry," Alec managed. "My God. I never knew he would go to such lengths. I should never have let you fight him. I should have—"

"Son... listen ... to .... me," Cinead said, struggling to get his words out.

"Father, dinna talk. Breathe. I'm here."

But Cinead plundered on. "Do not go ... after them. It is yer ... home ... now. Take care of ... the girls. I am ... proud of you."

With the last words, the air from Cinead's lungs escaped his body, and he fell limp into the moist grass behind him. Jaime let out a sob from behind him, and as much as Alec yearned to turn toward her, to run into her arms and let her hold him until the pain turned into a numb void, it was a luxury that he would never have.

Most certainly, not anymore.

Alec stood and looked around at the group, the men all taking a knee in honor of the man who was not just a fallen clan member but had been their laird, their leader, their guide. Roles which now all fell to Alec. The first responsibility coming now, far sooner than he would ever have wished for it.

He wasn't ready. But he didn't have much of a choice. He stopped and picked his father up, holding him in his arms.

"We have a burial to arrange," he said stoically to the other men before walking toward the barn.

* * *

The wake lasted only four days, as the weather was beginning to change and they needed to do the burial before the ground hardened. Every day Jaime did all she could to keep the house in order and look after Una and Hilda. Every night Jaime went to bed, alone.

Alec refused to allow anyone else to watch over the body, nor would he stay in her presence for any amount of time. Whenever she walked into a room, he left as though by closing himself off from her, he could keep himself from his grief.

On the third night after the Gillie attack, Jaime walked out to the barn to check on Alec and found him on his knees praying at his father's side. When he saw her, he spoke not a word, but instead walked over and shut the doors in her face, as he had fallen so deep into his grief, and likely, his guilt. He had drawn away from her, and Jaime began to feel as if she had made the wrong decision for staying here in this time, for following along with Alec's plan. She knew Alec blamed both of them, and she felt it along with him, if only he would share it with her.

On the fourth night of the mourning, the MacDermonts held a party to celebrate the life of their chieftain. It was both sorrowful and merry, as the clan ate, drank, and danced long into the night. The music could be heard for miles, and Jaime kept to the side of the celebrations, watching as the men drank more than college boys at frat parties – and they held the alcohol much better as well.

Jaime understood the importance of coming together and celebrating, but it was difficult when Alec was so withdrawn, so absent – from her, yes, but from all of his clan as well. A clan who needed him. And there were none who needed him more than his sisters.

Every night after Cinead's death, long after Jaime had tucked the girls into bed, Hilda would sneak into the bedroom and curl up next to Jaime, twirling her hair between her tiny fingers. Jaime's heart broke for the girls, but there was nothing she could do but be there for them, to try to fill the void that their mother, father and now Alec had left.

"Why won't Alec talk to us?" Hilda asked softly one night as she lay next to Jaime, and Jaime struggled to find the right words to answer her. "Is he mad at us?"

"Oh, sweetheart, no, not at all," Jaime said, needing the girl to understand that there was nothing she could ever do differently. "We all grieve in our own way, and Alec has taken this burden on his shoulders. I think he feels that it is all his fault, and he is having difficulty forgiving himself. He'll be back. It just might take some time."

Hilda nodded, but Jaime knew that for the rest of her life she would never forget the look of sadness on the little girl's face.

Alec's solemn behavior continued long after the funeral and Jaime waited patiently for weeks to bring up going to Crieff to look for the portal. Each day had a rhythm as she took care of the girls and learned to manage the household. She ensured everything was prepared each morning for Alec and Balloch before they departed for the day to work around the land in preparation before the weather truly turned. She would prepare their food and pack their meals so they wouldn't have to return for the midday meal. She thought they appreciated it, but they didn't say much.

In the evening the five of them would sit around the large dining table, eating in near silence but for the conversation Jaime forced. The girls would answer softly, while Alec would grunt out one-word answers. On the nights Balloch was there, he would enter the conversation, but he was often out with friends or local women.

The space between Alec and Jaime through the night was

like another person in the bed. Jaime longed for Alec to respond, but knew whatever was going on inside of him needed to work itself out. Alec would smile absently at Jaime from time to time, or kiss her on the forehead, but most days he sat, ate, and worked in silence.

Then one morning, four weeks after Cinead's death, Jaime woke with a strange feeling, as if there was an invisible shimmer in the air, some kind of sign that her life was about to change… again. Alec was already up, fastening his plaid on the other side of the room.

"Good morning," Jaime said tentatively, and he nodded at her without turning around.

"Morning," he muttered, and the ball of tense unease in her stomach only tightened. It seemed that when Cinead had died, so had a piece of Alec, a piece that Jaime desperately missed, even though she knew that she would have to let go of him soon anyway – if the day ever came.

She wondered what the point of all of this had been. Why would she have found her way back here in time, if it was only to cause chaos for the people who lived here? Had it all just been one big accident?

"Where are you going?" she asked, and when Alec pretended he hadn't heard her, she repeated her question. "Where are you going?"

"Out."

"Alec," she said as patiently as she could. She was aware that he probably wouldn't take kindly to his wife questioning him, but she had a bad feeling about this. "Are you going to seek revenge for your father?"

He stopped as he was about to put his sword in the holster but still didn't turn to look at her.

"It doesna matter."

"It does," she insisted, forcing herself out of the cozy

comfort of the bed and coming around to look at him. "You canna get yourself killed. The girls canna be left alone."

"Have more faith, Jaime," he muttered before breaking his fast and walking out the door, leaving Jaime staring after him.

CHAPTER 12

At dinner, Alec and Balloch returned with some goods they'd traded for in town. They set them down in the kitchen and joined the girls for dinner. Hilda talked about her day and a new hiding place she had found, while Una described the blanket she was going to begin knitting. When the plates were empty, Alec cleared his throat.

"Jaime and I are going to take a little trip tomorrow," Alec stated, looking up at Jaime. "We are going to be traveling to Crieff. I want you girls to look after the house. Balloch will stay close to keep an eye on you."

Jaime's eyes flew up to Alec's face in surprise.

"In the winter?" Hilda protested. "Ye'll freeze before you get there."

"We're gonna take the horses, so we won't have to camp," Alec responded. "We'll be leavin' when the sun comes up. I'll be back the next day before you go to bed."

The tension in the room was palpable, and the girls protested no further although Jaime could see Hilda's bottom lip was trembling while Una held her shoulders tightly back, as though she was trying to keep herself strong and together.

A TIME TO WED

Jaime walked them to their bedrooms and kissed each of them lightly, knowing it might be the last time she saw them. Her eyes filled with tears as she did everything she could to keep them from falling until she reached her own bedroom.

"Jaime," Hilda called out before she could walk away.

"Yes, Hilda?" Jaime responded.

"I love ye," she stated sleepily.

"I love you too, Hilda, and you as well, Una," Jaime replied, holding back her tears until she'd left the room. "So much. Sweet dreams."

When Jaime returned to the bedroom, Alec was in bed, his back to her and the door, likely fast asleep by now. Jaime curled into a ball on her side, her back to him, as the tears began to flow.

She had been here too long. She'd had too much time to form attachments, to consider these people family who she now loved as much as she had her own parents, in her own time. Yet how could it be possible that she should make a life here? Wasn't there a reason each person was born in their own time? She had her home, her friends, her running water. But nothing meant more to her than family. Maybe... but no. Had Alec given her any idea that he wanted her, that she belonged to him, his clan, then she could, perhaps, be convinced to stay. But it was clear that while he might still care for her, he wanted nothing more to do with her and likely regretted the fact he had ever come upon her in Crieff's Pass.

Jaime tried to cry silently, she truly did, but she still must have woken Alec, for she jumped when his hand came to her shoulder and he kissed her softly on the head.

"Thank you," Jaime whispered, longing to turn around and ask him to take her into his arms, but not wanting to be denied or, even worse, have him do so out of a sense of duty even if he had no wish to.

"Get some sleep, for 'tis a long ride to Crieff, tomorrow" Alec said as he blew out the lantern and turned around, pulling the blanket over top of them. "A promise is a promise."

Jaime lay in bed, staring up at the ceiling above her. She didn't know how to tell Alec how much she needed him, how they should take this last opportunity together and share in the love they once had. But all that reached her ears was tense silence, and Jaime thought her heart was shattering in her chest when Alec's light snore began to reverberate through the room.

She couldn't stay, not for a man who didn't want her, she reminded herself as she lay in the darkness, unable to sleep. She was making the right decision.

So why did it feel so wrong?

CHAPTER 13

The next morning everything moved quickly, and Alec was ready to leave before the sun had breached the horizon. Groggy from lack of sleep, Jaime put on the dress Alec had bought her when they first met and flung a wool-lined, hooded cloak around her shoulders to stay warm. After pulling Hilda and Una in for a long, tight hug, she told them again how much she loved them before she slipped on her gloves and walked out of the house, turning back for just a moment to remember it as it was, the majestic building that would likely be in ruins, if not completely disappeared, in her time. Guilt at being another adult to leave the girls wound through her heart and soul as they took off on their horses, trying to make Crieff before it got too dark outside, as the winters here were harsh.

They rode all day, breaking only once to eat and rest. Even when they stopped, Alec seemed somber but not as distant as he had been all these weeks. Perhaps it was because he was looking forward to seeing the last of her, Jaime thought wryly as she watched him re-pack the saddlebags before he helped her up onto her horse. He tapped her leg sweetly before walking back over and heading on toward the town. They would stay at the inn in Crieff and get up early to look for the portal in the light of the day.

By the time the sun had set, they could see Crieff and made their way into town, stopping where they had stayed before. They were both exhausted from the trip, so after they washed away the travel and started a fire, they snuggled into the bed and fell asleep quickly. The crackling from the fireplace woke Jaime several times, and she moved her head to lay on top of Alec's chest like she used to do. She tensed for a moment, wondering if he would push her away, but relaxed into him when he reached his arm over and rubbed her back as she fell back to sleep.

When Jaime woke in the morning, she found a note from Alec telling her he had gone into the town and she was to meet him out front when she was ready. She dressed and pulled her bag out, looking at all she had kept tucked away within it. It was shocking to her how being without the comforts of the future were not all that hard to get used to. In fact, she appreciated the lack of constant rings and notifications from text messages and emails. Jaime shook her head and shoved her belongings back in the bag before making her way downstairs. The sun was shining brightly, as it had been the day she'd arrived, and Jaime stopped for a moment, closing her eyes and letting the warmth of it seep through her.

"I'd know that dress anywhere," a nasally voice stated from in front of Jaime.

"Miss Fiona," Jaime said in a rush of shocked excitement, her words coming out in a rush at finding the woman who had been at the start of this entire mystery. Now that she had more clarity on where – and when – she was, aware that this wasn't a convoluted dream of her own making, she had questions for the woman. "What a wonderful surprise. I have so much to ask you. Please tell me, how did this happen? Why did I come here, to this time? And how do I get home?"

"Sometimes, child, ye need to figure out the whys of things for yerself," Fiona responded, her eyes looking much wiser than her age. "All I can do is help ye find yerself in the right place, at the right time."

"What are you, a fairy godmother or something?" Jaime said with a bit of a laugh.

"Call me what ye'd like child," Fiona replied. "Do ye ever feel someone is watching out for ye? Everyone feels that from time to time. But not everyone has me. I'm a bit more… hands on than most. Where ye headin'?" she asked, squinting through her glasses.

"Home," Jaime said resolutely. "If I can determine how to get there. But what —"

"Did ye take in the history?" she asked.

"More than you know," Jaime stated, looking down at her bag.

"Sometimes when yer heart is searching for something, time is of no consequence," Fiona said softly.

"Yes but —"

"Ye ready lass?" Alec asked, turning Jaime's attention away from Fiona and back toward the street in front of her.

"Oh, yes," Jaime said. "Just a moment, I need to finish talking to…."

Jaime turned toward Fiona, but when she did, the woman was gone. Jaime looked all around her and down the street before them, but it was like she had disappeared into thin air. Finally, Jaime's gaze rested on Alec, who was looking at her with raised eyebrows as if she had truly gone crazy this time. Jaime shook her head and began down the stairs, following

Alec out of the town and across the field to the woods. Before she crossed the threshold of the forest, she looked back at Crieff, wondering what would happen to the little town over the next five hundred years, wishing she could see it's progression from the town it was in this time to what it would become in hers.

Alec and Jaime walked for hours through Crieff's Pass, combing the area as they searched for any sign of a magical portal, or even the location that seemed familiar. Jaime knew Alec was still wondering if the quest was worthwhile, but he never uttered a word of complaint. The sun was shining down through the trees, casting beams of light like a cathedral ceiling. Three deer crossed their path, pausing just a moment to watch them before leaping off into the woods. Alec stopped and looked up at the sun and then around him in all directions before nodding resolutely.

"It's here," he said, his hands on his hips. "This is where I found ye," he said, looking out at the spot where he had first seen her lying in the mud.

They walked slowly over to the spot but only found a patch of fern. They began to look around the area, kicking leaves and rolling old fallen trees. Jaime wished she knew what she was looking for, but the truth was, it could be anything. She was peering out over the edge of a small cliff when she heard Alec call out.

"Jaime, it's – it's here," he said, incredulously. "I dinna believe it, but I found it."

Jaime ran over to him, a sudden whirring filling her ears as she stopped right at the edge of the dark swirling hole in the damp of the forest floor. It was a portal if she'd ever seen one, but as much as she had been looking for it, she was suddenly terrified. How could she jump into it? How could she leave him? Leave the girls? Her heart fluttered desperately, and she turned to Alec with so much that she needed to say to him, but the right words wouldn't come.

"Jaime." He spoke before she did, an ache in his voice that both shocked her and touched something deep within her. "I dinner ken how to thank you for all ye did for me, for my family." So that's what this was. A thank you. Jaime sighed and turned to go.

He must have sensed the movement, for he reached out a hand. "Jaime, please. Wait, just a moment. I- I know I put you in an impossible situation, took advantage of yer confusion, and yet, you did all I asked of you. Then when me father died... I blamed myself for not following along with his plan. But the truth is, had I done so, both he and I would be dead anyway. I was a boor to you, and I-I just need you to know how sorry I am. I should never have run from you, Jaime, but it all hurt so much, and I kept meself away from you as I knew that the closer I came, the more it would hurt when you left me."

"It's all behind us now," Jaime said, holding her breath and waiting for him to say something more, though what she wasn't sure. He had a point. She wished she had kept her feelings much more guarded, and then her heart wouldn't be breaking into pieces as it was in this moment. But she couldn't stay, wouldn't stay, for someone who didn't love her, as much as she had come to love him. For she did. She loved this Highland warrior, and yet he seemed to feel nothing than a bit of affection toward her. It wasn't enough.

"I guess this is goodbye, then," she said, her voice just above a whisper.

They looked at each other for a moment before Alec nodded curtly, and then turned and began to walk away, taking with him Jaime's heart. Jaime peered down toward the portal, barely able to see it anymore amidst the tears that had filled her eyes and were now pouring down her face. She took a breath as her attention shifted to a red-tailed fox that was scurrying away from across the portal. She closed her eyes, shutting out everything around her, as she began to countdown from five, convincing herself to jump in when she reached one.

"Jaime, stop!" Alec called out in the distance, his voice cutting through her misery, and Jaime's eyes flew open as she heard the quick pattern of his feet swiftly running toward her through the forest floor as he retraced his steps back to where he left her.

Had he forgotten something? Did he need more of her? Jaime wasn't sure she could take anymore, and she would have jumped into the portal and out of his reach, had it not been for that one small piece of her heart that still desperately hoped for his response. Alec reached her before her internal battle came to an end, and he took her arm and turned her toward him.

"Dinna go. Please. There, I said it. I've been a fool, Jaime. For I—I love you. I love ye more than anything. You've been nothing but patient, and loving, caring for my house and my family, and for me, when I've done nothing but push you away. You did all I asked without question, and I cannot imagine a woman who would better fit me, or my life, than you. I know ye've likely got much waiting for you in your century, and if I knew you had family or parents waiting for you there, I would never ask this of you. But there is one thing I can give you that your century cannot – family. And me, if you'll have me. I beg of ye, we need you. *I* need you. Stay with me."

The flow of Jaime's tears changed from a steady stream to a choking sob. She let out a deep breath of air as she tried to control herself and lifted a foot.

Only, she didn't step forward and into the portal. Instead,

she turned to the side and launched herself forward, into Alec's arms. They fastened their arms around one another, as he let out all of the air in his lungs, relaxing his head into her. She pressed her cheek against his chest, listening to his heart beating rapidly. He leaned down and kissed her on the lips in a move of pure possession as he pulled her close. The ball of nerves in her stomach since the day of the Gillie attack finally settled, and the yearning of her heart that had been reaching for something since the day she sat and stewed in her living room chair for hours finally found what it was looking for.

"Alec — I love you too," she whispered in his ear. "And I think I figured it out."

"You figured what out?" he asked pulling back.

"It wasn't Scotland calling to me all these years," she said, taking his face in her hands. "It was you. I was looking everywhere to try to find where I belonged, but it doesn't matter where I am or even what time I'm in. It's who I'm with. With you, I'm home."

"Does that mean... you will stay?"

Jaime nodded her head enthusiastically. "I will stay."

Alec hugged Jaime tightly once again, lifting her feet from the ground as he spun her in a circle. When he set her down, he clasped her hand, holding it tightly in his, as though if he let go, she would change her mind and run away from him, back to the portal. Before they reached the path, Jaime stopped and looked back.

"What is it?" Alec asked.

"I just have to do one thing," she said, her lips curling up into a smile at the panic that crossed his face. "Don't worry, I'll be right back.

She took off at a sprint to the portal, stopping when she reached the swirling black hole. As she looked into it, she knew she was right where she needed to be. Jaime took the leather bag from her shoulder, hugged it tightly against her chest, and then tossed it forward into the portal, which closed around it, the space where it had been returning to forest floor. She didn't need all those things. She had everything she needed right here.

EPILOGUE

The red, curly hair of the child flew behind her as she raced down the hill toward Jaime, who was waiting at the bottom. Jaime laughed as she caught her daughter and twirled her in a circle before she carried her back to the blanket, where Alec, Una and Hilda were waiting. They were due back shortly to meet Balloch and his new wife for dinner.

Jaime smiled to herself as she looked around her, at her family backdropped by the beautiful Scottish countryside. She had never been happier. Sure, she missed running water, and Danishes, and when she had given birth, she would have been much less fearful in a hospital with modern medicine, but she'd survived.

As much as she had given up, she had gained so much more. She wouldn't trade her life now for anything. She loved Alec with her entire heart, and at the birth of their child, her heart had grown even more to include their little girl, whom they named Mary, after Jaime's mother. Then there was Una and Hilda who were now as much like her daughters as Mary was.

She was whole. She had found what she was looking for, here in Scotland in the 16th century.

Alec reached out and ran a finger down her cheek, bringing her out of her thoughts and back to the moment.

"I love ye, lass," he said as he seemed to have picked up on her contemplative mood, for he swooped down and planted a kiss on her lips.

"I love you too, Alec," she responded as she leaned into him, brushing a hand over his stubbled cheek.

When the girls were tired from a day of playing in the sun, they packed up the blanket and returned home. Jaime smiled to herself. Not even in her craziest dream would she have imagined that home would be found five hundred years in the past.

After supper with Balloch and his wife, who was as large as Balloch was thin and the perfect match for him, Jaime and Alec put the girls to bed and retired to their room. Jaime was slightly melancholy tonight, as she realized before long it would be Una who would be married and leaving home. She was set to marry the son of a neighboring clan laird. Jaime had assured herself that he was a man — well, a boy really — who Una would be happy with. From the way Una's face blushed bright pink at the mere mention of his name, Jaime had been convinced it was a good match for the sweet girl, even if Jaime still thought Una was far too young to be married.

"'Tis the way it is, lass," said Alec, brushing her hair out of her eyes and away from her face. He had come into the room to find her standing there lost in her thoughts, and had coaxed her into telling him what was the matter. "She willna be going far, and he's a good lad. We'll still have Hilda at home, and Mary of course."

"Oh, I am happy for her, Alec, truly I am. Everything will be so different, though."

"Different is not always bad, love."

"That's very true. How wise my husband is," she said with a laugh.

"I have a year or two on ye, you know, wife," he responded.

"Yes, over five hundred of them to be exact."

With that, he picked her up with ease and cleared the smile from her face with a possessive kiss that took her breath away. How amazing it was that a touch from this man could still send her reeling in a way that no one before him ever could.

His fingers drifted through the long tendrils of hair cascading down her back as he laid her down on the bed. His kiss turned hungrier as he pushed down the shoulders of her dress to access her breasts, teasing one nipple and then the next with first his fingers and then his mouth.

She sighed as he trailed kisses down the side of her neck, and reached her hands underneath him to undo the tartan and slide it off. There was certainly more than one advantage to marrying a man in a kilt, she thought with a grin.

Alec freed her of her dress and tossed it behind him, grunting in appreciation of her naked body beneath him. He readied her for him with his fingers, then slid inside of her, finding home. His hand splayed behind her back as he thrust into her, whispering tender words into her ear. She would never, ever grow tired of this. How could she? She thought as his rhythmic lovemaking reached a crescendo, and they came together in an outpouring of love.

Afterwards, they lay together, their clothing a pool on the floor and sweat glistening off their bodies.

"Do ye ever miss it?" Alec said, breaking the silence.

"The future?" Jaime asked, raising a brow, for there couldn't be anything else he might be referring to.

"Aye."

"I could go for some Burger King right now," she said.

"What King is this?"

"It's a type of food," she said, laughing. "There are conveniences I miss, and some friends I would love to see again, but Alec, nothing will ever take me away from you."

He looked over at her.

"Do ye believe in fate? Or destiny?"

"I didn't before, but I think I do now. I think there are forces on this earth that we can't explain, things that happen to bring people together who are meant to be."

"I agree with ye, lass. There are some things that can never be explained, 'tis true, however I dinna want them to be. 'Tis easier to live without questioning everything good that happens, but rather to embrace it."

"Why Alec, the knowledge is pouring out of you tonight, my Highland warrior turned philosopher."

"Don' ye forget it, lass."

"Alec?" Jaime said, resting her head in the middle of his chest so as to hear his heart beat. "There is a reason I was thinking of change tonight."

"Oh?" he responded, stroking her hair.

"I'm pregnant again."

"You are with child?" he exclaimed as he sat up, catching her in his arms so that she wouldn't fall off of him. "Are ye sure?"

"Fairly sure. I mean, I can't be positive, not in the 16th century anyway, but all the signs are there. We're to have another baby!"

Happy tears fell from Jaime's eyes as Alec enveloped her in a strong but gentle hug, holding her softly against him.

"I canna imagine my life without you, lass," he said. "I shall never forget the moment you appeared to me, dropping to my feet at Crieff's Pass."

"Nor I without you," she replied. "Thank you for bringing me home."

* * *

THE END

* * *

Dear reader,

Welcome back to the present! I hope you enjoyed your journey back in time with Jaime. This series is something a little different for me, but I've always had a love of time travel. I wrote this series years ago, but recently decided to revisit and rewrite it. It was like my own trip back in time to visit characters that I have always loved.

This book is a trilogy, with the second trip back in time taking place in A Time to Love. There's a little teaser for you in the pages after this one, or you can head right to downloading it here.

If you haven't yet signed up for my newsletter, I would love to have you join us! You will receive Unmasking a Duke for free, as well as links to giveaways, sales, new releases, and stories about my coffee addiction, my struggle to keep my plants alive, and how much trouble one loveable wolf-lookalike dog can get into.

www.elliestclair.com/ellies-newsletter

Or you can join my Facebook group, Ellie St. Clair's Ever Afters, and stay in touch daily.

Until next time, happy reading!

With love,
Ellie

* * *

A Time to Dream
To the Time of the Highlander Book 2

Historian Emilia Guthrie has spent her life studying the past...what happens when that past comes to life?

While exploring the ruins of a Stonehaven castle, Emilia doesn't expect to see any signs of life – most especially an apparition of an injured Highland warrior. She can't help but follow where he leads, until she hurtles back through time to 16th century Scotland.

Dougal MacGavin has waited years to prove himself worthy to lead his clan as Laird. In the midst of avenging his father through a bloody battle, he must suddenly protect a woman as strange as she is beautiful.

Emilia is determined to save Dougal and the MacGavin clan, despite the fact he thinks her mad. How can they overcome their own battle of stubborn will and attraction to fight all that threatens to destroy them?

AN EXCERPT FROM A TIME TO LOVE

The sky was gray as Emilia hefted her heavy bag out of the cab and began rolling it into the JFK Airport.

She pushed her way through the typical New York City crowd, anxious to find her gate and be on her way.

Her phone dinged, and she stopped for a moment to check it, smiling when she saw it was the history dean, wishing her safe travels. She had been so grateful he had allowed her a couple of weeks' vacation before she assumed her new position. She knew it was a strange time to travel when she had so much to prepare, but she had been itching to visit the land she had studied for so long, and now that she had broken things off with Bryan, she felt somewhat… free.

Emilia had moved her belongings out the day after she told him about her new job, and was couching it at a friend's place until she could find a decent apartment close to work. She still cared for Bryan as a friend, but this new step forward in her life was the opportunity she needed to force herself to admit that he wasn't the love of her life. The fact that her tears had been few and her heart free instead of heavy confirmed the truth of it.

She found her gate to Aberdeenshire, Scotland, where she would hop off the plane and take a taxi to Stonehaven. She had wanted to visit Stonehaven for many years and had used to stare at the pictures online, wishing her life had been centered in that port city instead of the streaming metropolis around her. She couldn't wait to stand among the remains of old castles looking out over the ocean on the famous cliffs of Scotland. It was definitely better than scouring New York real estate to find somewhere she could afford and trying to ignore Bryan and his constant nagging about moving out the rest of her things.

She just couldn't deal with real life right now, and the only thing she felt like doing at the moment was leaving it all behind to visit the place where some of her ancestors had roamed, see the battlefields of the warring clans, and disappear from life for a bit into the world of her studies.

"Flight 6780 to Aberdeen, Scotland will be boarding in five minutes. Please have your tickets ready and your carry-ons tagged appropriately," the voice cracked over the speaker.

Emilia gathered her things and stood, walking over and waiting for them to call her section. She had already been through two security checks so she knew her bag was approved. All she really wanted to do was get into her seat, have a glass of whiskey, and relax. Boarding went quickly since the flight wasn't all that full, and Emilia strapped herself into her window seat, shoving her purse under the seat in front of her and taking a deep breath.

"Well, hello," a nasally voice said from the aisle seat across the empty middle.

"Hi," Emilia replied, smiling at the very loudly dressed woman sitting down next to her.

She was strange in a way Emilia couldn't quite put her finger on. Her hair was as red as Emilia's, but frizzy and wild, partially pulled back in a bun. She was wearing black-rimmed glasses, a bright multi-colored sweater, and didn't seem to be carrying anything, not even a purse. She smiled kindly as she sat rigidly and buckled up, leaning her head back against the seat with a nervous look in her eye. As the plane took off, she clasped the handles of her seat and Emilia turned toward the window, chastising herself for staring.

She could remember the first time she had ever flown. It was with her grandmother and they had, oddly enough, been visiting Scotland. For over a month, Emilia and her grandmother had traveled all across the country. That was when Emilia really started becoming interested in history, specifically Scottish history. Little did she know the trip was all a means to distract her eleven-year-old self from her parents' pending divorce. When she returned home, she dove into history, collecting all the books she could get her hands on, ignoring the drama going on around her.

As soon as the flight was in the air, Emilia ordered a double whiskey, threw in her headphones to avoid any awkward conversations, and zoned out. She watched as the plane traveled high over the ocean, everything below appearing so tiny and insignificant. She listened to a couple of songs on her playlist and then pulled out her laptop, deciding between a few old movies that she usually enjoyed. She finally chose *Grease*, her guilty pleasure. Another glass of whiskey later, she was fighting sleep. When the lights dimmed in the cabin and the sun outside of her window finished setting, it was game over. Emilia had been up for days, too worried and anxious about life to really sleep. But now, when relaxing was her only option, her body took over, and into the dream world she went.

Her dreams were wild, and oddly, the frazzled redheaded

woman beside her was in all of them. Emilia was traveling through some kind of portal and everything was black. She couldn't see or hear anything except the woman's voice, which kept repeating over and over again, "Listen to your heart." After what seemed like hours, Emilia could see a light approaching on the other end of the tunnel and as her feet touched down on the soft grass, she found herself in a very familiar Scotland, one she had studied for decades. Before she could look around or ask any questions, she was jolted awake by the landing of the plane.

Emilia squinted her eyes, trying to see around her, but she wasn't quite ready for the brightness of the sun was shining through the window. She took a deep breath and looked beside her, but the seat was empty. She furrowed her brow and looked up and down the aisle, but the woman with red hair seemed to have just vanished. She thought about asking the flight attendant, but by the time any of them were out of their seats, they were pulling up to the gate. Emilia shrugged her shoulders and pulled her carry-on out of the overhead before walking slowly out of the plane. While she waited for her luggage, she looked around her for the woman, but she was still nowhere to be seen. Strange.

Emilia collected her bags and headed out to find a car to take her to Stonehaven. Luckily, there were several taxis waiting out front, so she hopped in one and gave the address to the cottage she had rented by the ports. As the cab pulled out, she glanced over, startled to find her eyes lock with the mysterious woman from the plane. She was the only figure standing still amongst the moving crowd, smiling at Emilia as she passed in the taxi, as if she was there specifically to watch her. Emilia shook her head, figuring she must be going crazy, and decided it was better to focus on getting settled than wondering if she had finally reached a mental breakdown.

The drive was relaxing, and she completely forgot all about her worries as she passed through the beautiful rolling hills of Stonehaven. Off in the distance to her right peaked mountains that rose toward the sky, and to her left the beautiful ocean glittered like diamonds. Peace finally settled over her, and she sat back with a sigh of contentment, knowing she had made the right decision to come here. This trip definitely had everything she would need to get herself back on track.

When Emilia arrived at the cottage, she was almost giddy as she dragged her bags inside and left them in the entryway. She was too excited to worry about unpacking at the moment and immediately grabbed her notepad and set up her laptop.

Emilia was a planner, and she wanted to schedule every single moment of her trip to make sure she was able to really see everything she yearned to explore. There were more castles, remains, historical sites, and libraries on her list to visit than she could fit on one page.

She had two weeks but she didn't even think that would be enough time to really take in everything and still get a good sleep every night. She was like a kid on Christmas, unable to unwrap an unending pile of presents.

Emilia lit the fireplace to ward off the chill of the Scottish evenings and went through the cupboards to see what the cottage owners had stocked the kitchen with. She was pleased to find everything she had given them on her list, plus a ton of traditional Scottish dishes. One thing was certain, she definitely wouldn't go hungry while she was here. After making a warm cup of tea, she sat down in front of her laptop, staring at the pictures of Dunnottar Castle on the cliffs of Stonehaven. That was going to be her first castle visit, and she couldn't wait to see what her visit would reveal about its history.

* * *

Find A Time to Love on Amazon and in Kindle Unlimited!

ALSO BY ELLIE ST. CLAIR

To the Time of the Highlanders
A Time to Wed
A Time to Love
A Time to Dream

Thieves of Desire
The Art of Stealing a Duke's Heart
A Jewel for the Taking
A Prize Worth Fighting For
Gambling for the Lost Lord's Love
Romance of a Robbery

The Bluestocking Scandals
Designs on a Duke
Inventing the Viscount
Discovering the Baron
The Valet Experiment
Writing the Rake
Risking the Detective
A Noble Excavation
A Gentleman of Mystery

The Bluestocking Scandals Box Set: Books 1-4
The Bluestocking Scandals Box Set: Books 5-8

Blooming Brides

A Duke for Daisy

A Marquess for Marigold

An Earl for Iris

A Viscount for Violet

The Blooming Brides Box Set: Books 1-4

Happily Ever After

The Duke She Wished For

Someday Her Duke Will Come

Once Upon a Duke's Dream

He's a Duke, But I Love Him

Loved by the Viscount

Because the Earl Loved Me

Happily Ever After Box Set Books 1-3

Happily Ever After Box Set Books 4-6

The Victorian Highlanders

Duncan's Christmas - (prequel)

Callum's Vow

Finlay's Duty

Adam's Call

Roderick's Purpose

Peggy's Love

The Victorian Highlanders Box Set Books 1-5

Searching Hearts

Duke of Christmas (prequel)

Quest of Honor

Clue of Affection

Hearts of Trust

Hope of Romance

Promise of Redemption

Searching Hearts Box Set (Books 1-5)

Standalones

Always Your Love

The Stormswept Stowaway

A Touch of Temptation

Christmastide with His Countess

Her Christmas Wish

Merry Misrule

A Match Made at Christmas

For a full list of all of Ellie's books, please see www.elliestclair.com/books.

ABOUT THE AUTHOR

Ellie has always loved reading, writing, and history. For many years she has written short stories, non-fiction, and has worked on her true love and passion -- romance novels.

In every era there is the chance for romance, and Ellie enjoys exploring many different time periods, cultures, and geographic locations. No matter when or where, love can always prevail. She has a particular soft spot for the bad boys of history, and loves a strong heroine in her stories.

Ellie and her husband love nothing more than spending time at home with their children and Husky cross. Ellie can typically be found at the lake in the summer, pushing the stroller all year round, and, of course, with her computer in her lap or a book in hand.

She also loves corresponding with readers, so be sure to contact her!

www.elliestclair.com
ellie@elliestclair.com

Ellie St. Clair's Ever Afters Facebook Group

Printed in Great Britain
by Amazon